Stories of Mystery

Edited by Rossiter Johnson

Stories of Mystery

Copyright © 2022 Indo-European Publishing

The present edition is a reproduction of previous publication of this classic work. Minor typographical errors may have been corrected without note; however, for an authentic reading experience the spelling, punctuation, and capitalization have been retained from the original text.

ISBN: 978-1-64439-615-5

CONTENTS

THE GHOST

BY WILLIAM D. O'CONNOR

At the West End of Boston is a quarter of some fifty streets, more or less, commonly known as Beacon Hill.

It is a rich and respectable quarter, sacred to the abodes of Our First Citizens. The very houses have become sentient of its prevailing character of riches and respectability; and, when the twilight deepens on the place, or at high noon, if your vision is gifted, you may see them as long rows of Our First Giants, with very corpulent or very broad fronts, with solid-set feet of sidewalk ending in square-toed curbstone, with an air about them as if they had thrust their hard hands into their wealthy pockets forever, with a character of arctic reserve, and portly dignity, and a well-dressed, full-fed, self-satisfied, opulent, stony, repellent aspect to each, which says plainly, "I belong to a rich family, of the very highest respectability."

History, having much to say of Beacon Hill generally, has, on the present occasion, something to say particularly of a certain street which bends over the eminence, sloping steeply down to its base. It is an old street,—quaint, quiet, and somewhat picturesque. It was young once, though,—having been born before the Revolution, and was then given to the city by its father, Mr. Middlecott, who died without heirs, and did this much for posterity. Posterity has not been grateful to Mr. Middlecott. The street bore his name till he was dust, and then got the more aristocratic epithet of Bowdoin. Posterity has paid him by effacing what would have been his noblest epitaph. We may expect, after this, to see Faneuil Hall robbed of its name, and called Smith Hall! Republics are proverbially ungrateful. What safer claim to public remembrance has the old Huguenot, Peter Faneuil, than the old Englishman, Mr. Middlecott? Ghosts, it is said, have risen from the grave to reveal wrongs done them by the living; but it needs no ghost from the grave to prove the proverb about republics.

Bowdoin Street only differs from its kindred, in a certain shady, grave, old-fogy, fossil aspect, just touched with a pensive solemnity, as if it thought to itself, "I'm getting old, but I'm highly respectable;

1

that's a comfort." It has, moreover, a dejected, injured air, as if it brooded solemnly on the wrong done to it by taking away its original name and calling it Bowdoin; but as if, being a very conservative street, it was resolved to keep a cautious silence on the subject, lest the Union should go to pieces. Sometimes it wears a profound and mysterious look, as if it could tell something if it had a mind to, but thought it best not. Something of the ghost of its father—it was the only child he ever had!—walking there all the night, pausing at the corners to look up at the signs, which bear a strange name, and wringing his ghostly hands in lamentation at the wrong done his memory! Rumor told it in a whisper, many years ago. Perhaps it was believed by a few of the oldest inhabitants of the city; but the highly respectable quarter never heard of it, and, if it had, would not have been bribed to believe it, by any sum. Some one had said that some very old person had seen a phantom there. Nobody knew who some one was. Nobody knew who the very old person was. Nobody knew who had seen it, nor when, nor how. The very rumor was spectral.

All this was many years ago. Since then it has been reported that a ghost was seen there one bitter Christmas eve, two or three years back. The twilight was already in the street; but the evening lamps were not yet lighted in the windows, and the roofs and chimney-tops were still distinct in the last clear light of the dropping day. It was light enough, however, for one to read easily, from the opposite sidewalk, "Dr. C. Renton," in black letters, on the silver plate of a door, not far from the Gothic portal of the Swedenborgian church. Near this door stood a misty figure, whose sad, spectral eyes floated on vacancy, and whose long, shadowy white hair lifted like an airy weft in the streaming wind. That was the ghost! It stood near the door a long time, without any other than a shuddering motion, as though it felt the searching blast, which swept furiously from the north up the declivity of the street, rattling the shutters in its headlong passage. Once or twice, when a passer-by, muffled warmly from the bitter air, hurried past, the phantom shrank closer to the wall, till he was gone. Its vague, mournful face seemed to watch for some one. The twilight darkened gradually, but it did not flit away. Patiently it kept its piteous look fixed in one direction,—watching,—watching; and, while the howling wind swept frantically through the chill air, it still seemed to shudder in the piercing cold.

A light suddenly kindled in an opposite window. As if touched by a gleam from the lamp, or as if by some subtle interior illumination, the spectre became faintly luminous, and a thin smile seemed to quiver over its features. At the same moment, a strong, energetic figure—Dr. Renton himself—came in sight, striding down the slope of the pavement to his own door, his overcoat thrown back, as if the icy air were a tropical warmth to him, his hat set on the back of his head, and the loose ends of a 'kerchief about his throat, streaming in the nor'wester. The wind set up a howl the moment he came in sight, and swept upon him; and a curious agitation began on the part of the phantom. It glided rapidly to and fro, and moved in circles, and then, with the same swift, silent motion, sailed toward him, as if blown thither by the gale. Its long, thin arms, with something like a pale flame spiring from the tips of the slender fingers, were stretched out, as in greeting, while the wan smile played over its face; and when he rushed by, unheedingly, it made a futile effort to grasp the swinging arms with which he appeared to buffet back the buffeting gale. Then it glided on by his side, looking earnestly into his countenance, and moving its pallid lips with agonized rapidity, as if it said, "Look at me—speak to me—speak to me—see me!" But he kept his course with unconscious eyes, and a vexed frown on his forehead betokening an irritated mind. The light that had shone in the figure of the phantom darkened slowly, till the form was only a pale shadow. The wind had suddenly lulled, and no longer lifted its white hair. It still glided on with him, its head drooping on its breast, and its long arms hanging by its side; but when he reached the door, it suddenly sprang before him, gazing fixedly into his eyes, while a convulsive motion flashed over its grief-worn features, as if it had shrieked out a word. He had his foot on the step at the moment. With a start, he put his gloved hand to his forehead, while the vexed look went out quickly on his face. The ghost watched him breathlessly. But the irritated expression came back to his countenance more resolutely than before, and he began to fumble in his pocket for a latch-key, muttering petulantly, "What the devil is the matter with me now?" It seemed to him that a voice had cried clearly, yet as from afar, "Charles Renton!"—his own name. He had heard it in his startled mind; but then, he knew he was in a highly wrought state of nervous excitement, and his medical science, with that knowledge for a basis, could have reared a formidable fortress of explanation against any phenomenon, were it even more wonderful than this.

He entered the house; kicked the door to; pulled off his overcoat; wrenched off his outer 'kerchief; slammed them on a branch of the clothes-tree; banged his hat on top of them; wheeled about; pushed in the door of his library; strode in, and, leaving the door ajar, threw himself into an easy-chair, and sat there in the fire-reddened dusk, with his white brows knit, and his arms tightly locked on his breast. The ghost had followed him, sadly, and now stood motionless in a corner of the room, its spectral hands crossed on its bosom, and its white locks drooping down!

It was evident Dr. Renton was in a bad humor. The very library caught contagion from him, and became grouty and sombre. The furniture was grim and sullen and sulky; it made ugly shadows on the carpet and on the wall, in allopathic quantity; it took the red gleams from the fire on its polished surfaces in homœopathic globules, and got no good from them. The fire itself peered out sulkily from the black bars of the grate, and seemed resolved not to burn the fresh deposit of black coals at the top, but to take this as a good time to remember that those coals had been bought in the summer at five dollars a ton,—under price, mind you,—when poor people, who cannot buy at advantage, but must get their firing in the winter, would then have given nine or ten dollars for them. And so (glowered the fire), I am determined to think of that outrage, and not to light them, but to go out myself, directly! And the fire got into such a spasm of glowing indignation over the injury, that it lit a whole tier of black coals with a series of little explosions, before it could cool down, and sent a crimson gleam over the moody figure of its owner in the easy-chair, and over the solemn furniture, and into the shadowy corner filled by the ghost.

The spectre did not move when Dr. Renton arose and lit the chandelier. It stood there, still and gray, in the flood of mellow light. The curtains were drawn, and the twilight without had deepened into darkness. The fire was now burning in despite of itself, fanned by the wintry gusts, which found their way down the chimney. Dr. Renton stood with his back to it, his hands behind him, his bold white forehead shaded by a careless lock of black hair, and knit sternly; and the same frown in his handsome, open, searching dark eyes. Tall and strong, with an erect port, and broad, firm shoulders, high, resolute features, a commanding figure garbed in aristocratic black, and not yet verging into the proportions of obesity,—take him for all in all, a very fine and favorable specimen of the solid men of Boston. And seen in contrast (oh! could he but have known it!) with the attenuated figure of the poor, dim ghost!

Hark! a very light foot on the stairs,—a rich rustle of silks.

4

Everything still again,—Dr. Renton looking fixedly, with great sternness, at the half-open door, whence a faint, delicious perfume floats into the library. Somebody there, for certain. Somebody peeping in with very bright, arch eyes. Dr. Renton knew it, and prepared to maintain his ill-humor against the invader. His face became triply armed with severity for the encounter. That's Netty, I know, he thought. His daughter. So it was. In she bounded. Bright little Netty! Gay little Netty! A dear and sweet little creature, to be sure, with a delicate and pleasant beauty of face and figure, it needed no costly silks to grace or heighten. There she stood. Not a word from her merry lips, but a smile which stole over all the solitary grimness of the library, and made everything better, and brighter, and fairer, in a minute. It floated down into the cavernous humor of Dr. Renton, and the gloom began to lighten directly,— though he would not own it, nor relax a single feature. But the wan ghost in the corner lifted its head to look at her, and slowly brightened as to something worthy a spirit's love, and a dim phantom's smiles. Now then, Dr. Renton! the lines are drawn, and the foe is coming. Be martial, sir, as when you stand in the ranks of the Cadets on training-days! Steady, and stand the charge! So he did. He kept an inflexible front as she glided toward him, softly, slowly, with her bright eyes smiling into his, and doing dreadful execution. Then she put her white arms around his neck, laid her dear, fair head on his breast, and peered up archly into his stern visage. Spite of himself, he could not keep the fixed lines on his face from breaking confusedly into a faint smile. Somehow or other, his hands came from behind him, and rested on her head. There! That's all. Dr. Renton surrendered at discretion! One of the solid men of Boston was taken after a desperate struggle,—internal, of course,— for he kissed her, and said, "Dear little Netty!" and so she was.

The phantom watched her with a smile, and wavered and brightened as if about to glide to her; but it grew still, and remained.

"Pa in the sulks to-night?" she asked, in the most winning, playful, silvery voice.

"Pa's a fool," he answered in his deep chest-tones, with a vexed good-humor; "and you know it."

"What's the matter with pa? What makes him be a great bear? Papasy, dear," she continued, stroking his face with her little hands, and patting him, very much as Beauty might have patted the Beast after she fell in love with him; or as if he were a great baby. In fact, he began to look then as if he were.

"Matter? Oh! everything's the matter, little Netty. The world goes round too fast. My boots pinch. Somebody stole my umbrella last year. And I've got a headache." He concluded this fanciful abstract of his grievances by putting his arms around her, and kissing her again. Then he sat down in the easy-chair, and took her fondly on his knee.

"Pa's got a headache! It is t-o-o bad, so it is," she continued in the same soothing, winning way, caressing his brow with her tiny hands. "It's a horrid shame, so it is! P-o-o-r pa. Where does it ache, papa-sy, dear? In the forehead? Cerebrum or cerebellum, papa-sy? Occiput or sinciput, deary?"

"Bah! you little quiz," he replied, laughing and pinching her cheek, "none of your nonsense! And what are you dressed up in this way for, to-night? Silks, and laces, and essences, and what not! Where are you going, fairy?"

"Going out with mother for the evening, Dr. Renton," she replied briskly; "Mrs. Larrabee's party, papa-sy. Christmas eve, you know. And what are you going to give me for a present, to-morrow, pa-sy?"

"To-morrow will tell, little Netty."

"Good! And what are you going to give me, so that I can make my presents, Beary?"

"Ugh!" But he growled it in fun, and had a pocket-book out from his breast-pocket directly after. Fives—tens—twenties—fifties—all crisp, and nice, and new bank-notes.

"Will that be enough, Netty?" He held up a twenty. The smiling face nodded assent, and the bright eyes twinkled.

"No, it won't. But that will," he continued, giving her a fifty.

"Fifty dollars, Globe Bank, Boston!" exclaimed Netty, making great eyes at him. "But we must take all we can get, pa-sy; mustn't we? It's too much, though. Thank you all the same, pa-sy, nevertheless." And she kissed him, and put the bill in a little bit of a portemonnaie with a gay laugh.

6

"Well done, I declare!" he said, smilingly. "But you're going to the party?"

"Pretty soon, pa."

He made no answer; but sat smiling at her. The phantom watched them, silently.

"What made pa so cross and grim, to-night? Tell Netty—do," she pleaded.

"Oh! because;—everything went wrong with me, to-day. There." And he looked as sulky, at that moment, as he ever did in his life.

"No, no, pa-sy; that won't do. I want the particulars," continued Netty, shaking her head, smilingly.

"Particulars! Well, then, Miss Nathalie Renton," he began, with mock gravity, "your professional father is losing some of his oldest patients. Everybody is in ruinous good health; and the grass is growing in the graveyards."

"In the winter time, papa?—smart grass!"

"Not that I want practice," he went on, getting into soliloquy; "or patients, either. A rich man who took to the profession simply for the love of it, can't complain on that score. But to have an interloping she-doctor take a family I've attended ten years, out of my hands, and to hear the hodge-podge gabble about physiological laws, and woman's rights, and no taxation without representation, they learn from her,—well, it's too bad!"

"Is that all, pa-sy? Seems to me I'd like to vote, too," was Netty's piquant rejoinder.

"Hoh! I'll warrant," growled her father. "Hope you'll vote the Whig ticket, Netty, when you get your rights."

"Will the Union be dissolved, then, pa-sy,—when the Whigs are beaten?"

"Bah! you little plague," he growled, with a laugh. "But, then, you women don't know anything about politics. So, there. As I was saying, everything went wrong with me to-day. I've been speculating in railroad stock, and singed my fingers. Then, old Tom Hollis outbid me to-day, at Leonard's, on a rare medical work I had set my

7

eyes upon having. Confound him! Then, again, two of my houses are tenantless, and there are folks in two others that won't pay their rent, and I can't get them out. Out they'll go, though, or I'll know why. And, to crown all—um-m. And I wish the Devil had him! as he will."

"Had who, Beary-papa?"

"Him. I'll tell you. The street-floor of one of my houses in Hanover Street lets for an oyster-room. They keep a bar there, and sell liquor. Last night they had a grand row,—a drunken fight, and one man was stabbed, it's thought fatally."

"O father!" Netty's bright eyes dilated with horror.

"Yes. I hope he won't die. At any rate, there's likely to be a stir about the matter, and my name will be called into question, then, as I'm the landlord. And folks will make a handle of it, and there'll be the deuce to pay, generally."

He got back the stern, vexed frown, to his face, with the anticipation, and beat the carpet with his foot. The ghost still watched from the angle of the room, and seemed to darken, while its features looked troubled.

"But, father," said Netty, a little tremulously, "I wouldn't let my houses to such people. It's not right; is it? Why, it's horrid to think of men getting drunk, and killing each other!"

Dr. Renton rubbed his hair into disorder, with vexation, and then subsided into solemnity.

"I know it's not exactly right, Netty; but I can't help it. As I said before, I wish the Devil had that barkeeper. I ought to have ordered him out long ago, and then this wouldn't have happened. I've increased his rent twice, hoping to get rid of him so; but he pays without a murmur; and what am I to do? You see, he was an occupant when the building came into my hands, and I let him stay. He pays me a good, round rent; and, apart from his cursed traffic, he's a good tenant. What can I do? It's a good thing for him, and it's a good thing for me, pecuniarily. Confound him! Here's a nice rumpus brewing!"

"Dear pa, I'm afraid it's not a good thing for you," said Netty, caressing him and smoothing his tumbled hair. "Nor for him either.

8

I wouldn't mind the rent he pays you. I'd order him out. It's bad money. There's blood on it."

She had grown pale, and her voice quivered. The phantom glided over to them, and laid its spectral hand upon her forehead. The shadowy eyes looked from under the misty hair into the doctor's face, and the pale lips moved as if speaking the words heard only in the silence of his heart,—"Hear her, hear her!"

"I must think of it," resumed Dr. Renton, coldly. "I'm resolved, at all events, to warn him that if anything of this kind occurs again, he must quit at once. I dislike to lose a profitable tenant; for no other business would bring me the sum his does. Hang it, everybody does the best he can with his property,—why shouldn't I?"

The ghost, standing near them, drooped its head again on its breast, and crossed its arms. Netty was silent. Dr. Renton continued, petulantly,—

"A precious set of people I manage to get into my premises. There's a woman hires a couple of rooms for a dwelling, overhead, in that same building, and for three months I haven't got a cent from her. I know these people's tricks. Her month's notice expires to-morrow, and out she goes."

"Poor creature!" sighed Netty.

He knit his brow, and beat the carpet with his foot, in vexation.

"Perhaps she can't pay you, pa," trembled the sweet, silvery voice. "You wouldn't turn her out in this cold winter, when she can't pay you,—would you, pa?"

"Why don't she get another house, and swindle some one else?" he replied, testily; "there's plenty of rooms to let."

"Perhaps she can't find one, pa," answered Netty.

"Humbug!" retorted her father; "I know better."

"Pa, dear, if I were you, I'd turn out that rumseller, and let the poor woman stay a little longer; just a little, pa."

"Sha'n't do it. Hah! that would be scattering money out of both pockets. Sha'n't do it. Out she shall go; and as for him,—well, he'd better turn over a new leaf. There, let us leave the subject, darling. It vexes me. How did we contrive to get into this train? Bah!"

He drew her closer to him, and kissed her forehead. She sat quietly, with her head on his shoulder, thinking very gravely.

"I feel queerly to-day, little Netty," he began, after a short pause. "My nerves are all high-strung with the turn matters have taken."

"How is it, papa? The headache?" she answered.

"Y-e-s—n-o—not exactly; I don't know," he said dubiously; then, in an absent way, "it was that letter set me to think of him all day, I suppose."

"Why, pa, I declare," cried Netty, starting up, "if I didn't forget all about it, and I came down expressly to give it to you! Where is it? Oh! here it is."

She drew from her pocket an old letter, faded to a pale yellow, and gave it to him. The ghost started suddenly.

"Why, bless my soul! it's the very letter! Where did you get that, Nathalie?" asked Dr. Renton.

"I found it on the stairs after dinner, pa."

"Yes, I do remember taking it up with me; I must have dropped it," he answered, musingly, gazing at the superscription. The ghost was gazing at it, too, with startled interest.

"What beautiful writing it is, pa," murmured the young girl. "Who wrote it to you? It looks yellow enough to have been written a long time since."

"Fifteen years ago, Netty. When you were a baby. And the hand that wrote it has been cold for all that time."

He spoke with a solemn sadness, as if memory lingered with the heart of fifteen years ago, on an old grave. The dim figure by his side had bowed its head, and all was still.

"It is strange," he resumed, speaking vacantly and slowly, "I have not thought of him for so long a time, and to-day—especially this evening—I have felt as if he were constantly near me. It is a singular feeling."

He put his left hand to his forehead, and mused,—his right clasped his daughter's shoulder. The phantom slowly raised its head, and gazed at him with a look of unutterable tenderness.

"Who was he, father?" she asked with a hushed voice.

"A young man, an author, a poet. He had been my dearest friend, when we were boys; and, though I lost sight of him for years,—he led an erratic life,—we were friends when he died. Poor, poor fellow! Well, he is at peace."

The stern voice had saddened, and was almost tremulous. The spectral form was still.

"How did he die, father?"

"A long story, darling," he replied, gravely, "and a sad one. He was very poor and proud. He was a genius,—that is, a person without an atom of practical talent. His parents died, the last, his mother, when he was near manhood. I was in college then. Thrown upon the world, he picked up a scanty subsistence with his pen, for a time. I could have got him a place in the counting-house, but he would not take it; in fact, he wasn't fit for it. You can't harness Pegasus to the cart, you know. Besides, he despised mercantile life, without reason, of course; but he was always notional. His love of literature was one of the rocks he foundered on. He was n't successful; his best compositions were too delicate, fanciful, to please the popular taste; and then he was full of the radical and fanatical notions which infected so many people at that time in New England, and infect them now, for that matter; and his sublimated, impracticable ideas and principles, which he kept till his dying day, and which, I confess, alienated me from him, always staved off his chances of success. Consequently, he never rose above the drudgery of some employment on newspapers. Then he was terribly passionate, not without cause, I allow; but it wasn't wise. What I mean is this: if he saw, or if he fancied he saw, any wrong or injury done to any one, it was enough to throw him into a frenzy; he would get black in the face and absolutely shriek out his denunciations of the wrong-doer. I do believe he would have visited his own brother with the most unsparing invective, if that brother had laid a harming finger on a street-beggar, or a colored man, or a poor person of any kind. I don't blame the feeling; though with a man like him it was very apt to be a false or mistaken one; but, at any rate, its exhibition wasn't sensible. Well, as I was saying, he buffeted about in this world a long time, poorly paid, fed, and clad; taking more care of other

11

people than he did of himself. Then mental suffering, physical exposure, and want killed him."

The stern voice had grown softer than a child's. The same look of unutterable tenderness brooded on the mournful face of the phantom by his side; but its thin, shining hand was laid upon his head, and its countenance had undergone a change. The form was still undefined; but the features had become distinct. They were those of a young man, beautiful and wan, and marked with great suffering.

A pause had fallen on the conversation, in which the father and daughter heard the solemn sighing of the wintry wind around the dwelling. The silence seemed scarcely broken by the voice of the young girl.

"Dear father, this was very sad. Did you say he died of want?"

"Of want, my child, of hunger and cold. I don't doubt it. He had wandered about, as I gather, houseless for a couple of days and nights. It was in December, too. Some one found him, on a rainy night, lying in the street, drenched and burning with fever, and had him taken to the hospital. It appears that he had always cherished a strange affection for me, though I had grown away from him; and in his wild ravings he constantly mentioned my name, and they sent for me. That was our first meeting after two years. I found him in the hospital—dying. Heaven can witness that I felt all my old love for him return then, but he was delirious, and never recognized me. And, Nathalie, his hair,—it had been coal-black, and he wore it very long,—he wouldn't let them cut it either; and as they knew no skill could save him, they let him have his way,—his hair was then as white as snow! God alone knows what that brain must have suffered to blanch hair which had been as black as the wing of a raven!"

He covered his eyes with his hand, and sat silently. The fingers of the phantom still shone dimly on his head, and its white locks drooped above him, like a weft of light.

"What was his name, father?" asked the pitying girl.

"George Feval. The very name sounds like fever. He died on Christmas eve, fifteen years ago this night. It was on his death-bed, while his mind was tossing on a sea of delirious fancies, that he wrote me this long letter,—for to the last, I was uppermost in his thoughts. It is a wild, incoherent thing, of course,—a strange

12

mixture of sense and madness. But I have kept it as a memorial of him. I have not looked at it for years; but this morning I found it among my papers, and somehow it has been in my mind all day."

He slowly unfolded the faded sheets, and sadly gazed at the writing. His daughter had risen from her half-recumbent posture, and now bent her graceful head over the leaves. The phantom covered its face with its hands.

"What a beautiful manuscript it is, father!" she exclaimed. "The writing is faultless."

"It is, indeed," he replied. "Would he had written his life as fairly!"

"Read it, father," said Nathalie.

"No, but I'll read you a detached passage here and there," he answered, after a pause. "The rest you may read yourself some time, if you wish. It is painful to me. Here's the beginning:—

"'My Dear Charles Renton:—Adieu, and adieu. It is Christmas eve, and I am going home. I am soon to exhale from my flesh, like the spirit of a broken flower. Exultemus forever!'

• • • • •

"It is very wild. His mind was in a fever-craze. Here is a passage that seems to refer to his own experience of life:—

"'Your friendship was dear to me. I give you true love. Stocks and returns. You are rich, but I did not wish to be your bounty's pauper. Could I beg? I had my work to do for the world, but oh! the world has no place for souls that can only love and suffer. How many miles to Babylon? Threescore and ten. Not so far—not near so far! Ask starvelings—they know.

• • • • •

I wanted to do the world good, and the world has killed me, Charles.'"
• • • • •

"It frightens me," said Nathalie, as he paused.

13

"We will read no more," he replied sombrely. "It belongs to the psychology of madness. To me, who knew him, there are gleams of sense in it, and passages where the delirium of the language is only a transparent veil on the meaning. All the remainder is devoted to what he thought important advice to me. But it's all wild and vague. Poor—poor George!"

The phantom still hid its face in its hands, as the doctor slowly turned over the pages of the letter. Nathalie, bending over the leaves, laid her finger on the last, and asked, "What are those closing sentences, father? Read them."

"Oh! that is what he called his 'last counsel' to me. It's as wild as the rest,—tinctured with the prevailing ideas of his career. First he says, 'Farewell—farewell'; then he bids me take his 'counsel into memory on Christmas day'; then after enumerating all the wretched classes he can think of in the country, he says: 'These are your sisters and your brothers,—love them all.' Here he says, 'O friend, strong in wealth for so much good, take my last counsel. In the name of the Saviour, I charge you be true and tender to mankind.' He goes on to bid me 'live and labor for the fallen, the neglected, the suffering, and the poor'; and finally ends by advising me to help upset any, or all, institutions, laws, and so forth, that bear hardly on the fag-ends of society; and tells me that what he calls 'a service to humanity' is worth more to the doer than a service to anything else, or than anything we can gain from the world. Ah, well! poor George."

"But isn't all that true, father?" said Netty; "it seems so."

"H'm," he murmured through his closed lips. Then, with a vague smile, folding up the letter, meanwhile, he said, "Wild words, Netty, wild words. I've no objection to charity, judiciously given; but poor George's notions are not mine. Every man for himself, is a good general rule. Every man for humanity, as George has it, and in his acceptation of the principle, would send us all to the almshouse pretty soon. The greatest good of the greatest number,—that's my rule of action. There are plenty of good institutions for the distressed, and I'm willing to help support 'em, and do. But as for making a martyr of one's self, or tilting against the necessary evils of society, or turning philanthropist at large, or any quixotism of that sort, I don't believe in it. We didn't make the world, and we can't mend it. Poor George. Well—he's at rest. The world wasn't the place for him."

They grew silent. The spectre glided slowly to the wall, and stood as

14

if it were thinking what, with Dr. Renton's rule of action, was to become of the greatest good of the smallest number. Nathalie sat on her father's knee, thinking only of George Feval, and of his having been starved and grieved to death.

"Father," said Nathalie, softly, "I felt, while you were reading the letter, as if he were near us. Didn't you? The room was so light and still, and the wind sighed so."

"Netty, dear, I've felt that all day, I believe," he replied. "Hark! there is the door-bell. Off goes the spirit-world, and here comes the actual. Confound it! Some one to see me, I'll warrant, and I'm not in the mood."

He got into a fret at once. Netty was not the Netty of an hour ago, or she would have coaxed him out of it. But she did not notice it now in her abstraction. She had risen at the tinkle of the bell, and seated herself in a chair. Presently a nose, with a great pimple on the end of it, appeared at the edge of the door, and a weak, piping voice said, reckless of the proper tense, "There was a woman wanted to see you, sir."

"Who is it, James?—no matter, show her in."

He got up with the vexed scowl on his face, and walked the room. In a minute the library door opened again, and a pale, thin, rigid, frozen-looking little woman, scantily clad, the weather being considered, entered, and dropped a curt, awkward bow to Dr. Renton.

"O, Mrs. Miller! Good evening, ma'am. Sit down," he said, with a cold, constrained civility.

The little woman faintly said, "Good evening, Dr. Renton," and sat down stiffly, with her hands crossed before her, in the chair nearest the wall. This was the obdurate tenant, who had paid no rent for three months, and had a notice to quit, expiring to-morrow.

"Cold evening, ma'am," remarked Dr. Renton, in his hard way.

"Yes, sir, it is," was the cowed, awkward answer.

"Won't you sit near the fire, ma'am?" said Netty, gently; "you look cold."

"No, miss, thank you. I'm not cold," was the faint reply. She was

15

cold, though, as well she might be with her poor, thin shawl, and open bonnet, in such a bitter night as it was outside. And there was a rigid, sharp, suffering look in her pinched features that betokened she might have been hungry, too. "Poor people don't mind the cold weather, miss," she said, with a weak smile, her voice getting a little stronger. "They have to bear it, and they get used to it."

She had not evidently borne it long enough to effect the point of indifference. Netty looked at her with a tender pity. Dr. Renton thought to himself, Hoh!—blazoning her poverty,—manufacturing sympathy already,—the old trick; and steeled himself against any attacks of that kind, looking jealously, meanwhile, at Netty.

"Well, Mrs. Miller," he said, "what is it this evening? I suppose you've brought me my rent."

The little woman grew paler, and her voice seemed to fail on her quivering lips. Netty cast a quick, beseeching look at her father.

"Nathalie, please to leave the room." We'll have no nonsense carried on here, he thought, triumphantly, as Netty rose, and obeyed the stern, decisive order, leaving the door ajar behind her.

He seated himself in his chair, and resolutely put his right leg up to rest on his left knee. He did not look at his tenant's face, determined that her piteous expressions (got up for the occasion, of course) should be wasted on him.

"Well, Mrs. Miller," he said again.

"Dr. Renton," she began, faintly gathering her voice as she proceeded, "I have come to see you about the rent. I am very sorry, sir, to have made you wait, but we have been unfortunate."

"Sorry, ma'am," he replied, knowing what was coming; "but your misfortunes are not my affair. We all have misfortunes, ma'am. But we must pay our debts, you know."

"I expected to have got money from my husband before this, sir," she resumed, "and I wrote to him. I got a letter from him to-day, sir, and it said that he sent me fifty dollars a month ago, in a letter; and it appears that the post-office is to blame, or somebody, for I never got it. It was nearly three months' wages, sir, and it is very hard to lose it. If it had n't been for that your rent would have been paid long ago, sir."

16

"Don't believe a word of that story," thought Dr. Renton, sententiously.

"I thought, sir," she continued, emboldened by his silence, "that if you would be willing to wait a little longer, we would manage to pay you soon, and not let it occur again. It has been a hard winter with us, sir; firing is high, and provisions, and everything; and we're only poor people, you know, and it's difficult to get along."

The doctor made no reply.

"My husband was unfortunate, sir, in not being able to get employment here," she resumed; "his being out of work in the autumn, threw us all back, and we've got nothing to depend on but his earnings. The family that he's in now, sir, don't give him very good pay,—only twenty dollars a month, and his board,—but it was the best chance he could get, and it was either go to Baltimore with them, or stay at home and starve, and so he went, sir. It's been a hard time with us, and one of the children is sick, now, with a fever, and we don't hardly know how to make out a living. And so, sir, I have come here this evening, leaving the children alone, to ask you if you wouldn't be kind enough to wait a little longer, and we'll hope to make it right with you in the end."

"Mrs. Miller," said Dr. Renton, with stern composure, "I have no wish to question the truth of any statement you may make; but I must tell you plainly, that I can't afford to let my houses for nothing. I told you a month ago, that if you couldn't pay me my rent, you must vacate the premises. You know very well that there are plenty of tenants who are able and willing to pay when the money comes due. You know that."

He paused as he said this, and, glancing at her, saw her pale lips falter. It shook the cruelty of his purpose a little, and he had a vague feeling that he was doing wrong. Not without a proud struggle, during which no word was spoken, could he beat it down. Meanwhile, the phantom had advanced a pace toward the centre of the room.

"That is the state of the matter, ma'am," he resumed, coldly. "People who will not pay me my rent must not live in my tenements. You must move out. I have no more to say."

"Dr. Renton," she said, faintly, "I have a sick child,—how can I move now? O, sir, it's Christmas eve,—don't be hard with us!"

17

Instead of touching him, this speech irritated him beyond measure. Passing all considerations of her difficult position involved in her piteous statement, his anger flashed at once on her implication that he was unjust and unkind. So violent was his excitement that it whirled away the words that rushed to his lips, and only fanned the fury that sparkled from the whiteness of his face in his eyes.

"Be patient with us, sir," she continued; "we are poor, but we mean to pay you; and we can't move now in this cold weather; please, don't be hard with us, sir."

The fury now burst out on his face in a red and angry glow, and the words came.

"Now, attend to me!" He rose to his feet. "I will not hear any more from you. I know nothing of your poverty, nor of the condition of your family. All I know is that you owe me three months' rent, and that you can't or won't pay me. I say, therefore, leave the premises to people who can and will. You have had your legal notice; quit my house to-morrow; if you don't, your furniture shall be put in the street. Mark me,—to-morrow!"

The phantom had rushed into the centre of the room. Standing face to face with him,—dilating,—blackening,—its whole form shuddering with a fury to which his own was tame,—the semblance of a shriek upon its flashing lips, and on its writhing features, and an unearthly anger streaming from its bright and terrible eyes,—it seemed to throw down, with its tossing arms, mountains of hate and malediction on the head of him whose words had smitten poverty and suffering, and whose heavy hand was breaking up the barriers of a home.

Dr. Renton sank again into his chair. His tenant,—not a woman!—not a sister in humanity!—but only his tenant; she sat crushed and frightened by the wall. He knew it vaguely. Conscience was battling in his heart with the stubborn devils that had entered there. The phantom stood before him, like a dark cloud in the image of a man. But its darkness was lightening slowly, and its ghostly anger had passed away.

The poor woman, paler than before, had sat mute and trembling, with all her hopes ruined. Yet her desperation forbade her to abandon the chances of his mercy, and she now said,—

"Dr. Renton, you surely don't mean what you have told me. Won't

18

you bear with me a little longer, and we will yet make it all right with you?"

"I have given you my answer," he returned, coldly; "I have no more to add. I never take back anything I say—never!"

It was true. He never did—never! She half rose from her seat as if to go; but weak and sickened with the bitter result of her visit, she sunk down again with her head bowed. There was a pause. Then, solemnly gliding across the lighted room, the phantom stole to her side with a glory of compassion on its wasted features. Tenderly, as a son to a mother, it bent over her; its spectral hands of light rested upon her in caressing and benediction; its shadowy fall of hair, once blanched by the anguish of living and loving, floated on her throbbing brow; and resignation and comfort not of this world sank upon her spirit, and consciousness grew dim within her, and care and sorrow seemed to die.

He who had been so cruel and so hard, sat silent in black gloom. The stern and sullen mood, from which had dropped but one fierce flash of anger, still hung above the heat of his mind, like a dark rack of thundercloud. It would have burst anew into a fury of rebuke, had he but known his daughter was listening at the door, while the colloquy went on. It might have flamed violently, had his tenant made any further attempt to change his purpose. She had not. She had left the room meekly, with the same curt, awkward bow that marked her entrance. He recalled her manner very indistinctly; for a feeling like a mist began to gather in his mind, and make the occurrences of moments before uncertain.

Alone, now, he was yet oppressed with a sensation that something was near him. Was it a spiritual instinct? for the phantom stood by his side. It stood silent, with one hand raised above his head, from which a pale flame seemed to flow downward to his brain; its other hand pointed movelessly to the open letter on the table beside him.

He took the sheets from the table, thinking, at the moment, only of George Feval; but the first line on which his eye rested was, "In the name of the Saviour, I charge you, be true and tender to mankind!" And the words touched him like a low voice from the grave. Their penetrant reproach pierced the hardness of his heart. He tossed the letter back on the table. The very manner of the act accused him of an insult to the dead. In a moment he took up the faded sheets more reverently, but only to lay them down again.

19

He had not been well that day, and he now felt worse than before. The pain in his head had given place to a strange sense of dilation, and there was a silent, confused riot in his fevered brain, which seemed to him like the incipience of insanity. Striving to divert his mind from what had passed, by reflection on other themes, he could not hold his thoughts; they came teeming but dim, and slipped and fell away; and only the one circumstance of his recent cruelty, mixed with remembrance of George Feval, recurred and clung with vivid persistence. This tortured him. Sitting there, with arms tightly interlocked, he resolved to wrench his mind down by sheer will upon other things; and a savage pleasure at what at once seemed success, took possession of him. In this mood, he heard soft footsteps and the rustle of festal garments on the stairs, and had a fierce complacency in being able to apprehend clearly that it was his wife and daughter going out to the party. In a moment he heard the controlled and even voice of Mrs. Renton,—a serene and polished lady with whom he had lived for years in cold and civil alienation, both seeing as little of each other as possible. With a scowl of will upon his brow, he received her image distinctly into his mind, even to the minutia of the dress and ornaments he knew she wore, and felt an absolutely savage exultation in his ability to retain it. Then came the sound of the closing of the hall door and the rattle of receding wheels, and somehow it was Nathalie and not his wife that he was holding so grimly in his thought, and with her, salient and vivid as before, the tormenting remembrance of his tenant, connected with the memory of George Feval. Springing to his feet, he walked the room.

He had thrown himself on a sofa, still striving to be rid of his remorseful visitations, when the library door opened, and the inside man appeared, with his hand held bashfully over his nose. It flashed on him at once that his tenant's husband was the servant of a family like this fellow; and, irritated that the whole matter should be thus broadly forced upon him in another way, he harshly asked him what he wanted. The man only came in to say that Mrs. Renton and the young lady had gone out for the evening, but that tea was laid for him in the dining-room. He did not want any tea, and if anybody called, he was not at home. With this charge, the man left the room, closing the door behind him.

If he could but sleep a little! Rising from the sofa, he turned the lights of the chandelier low, and screened the fire. The room was still. The ghost stood, faintly radiant, in a remote corner. Dr. Renton lay down again, but not to repose. Things he had forgotten of his dead friend, now started up again in remembrance, fresh from the grave of many years; and not one of them but linked itself by some mysterious bond to something connected with his tenant, and became an accusation.

He had lain thus for more than an hour, feeling more and more unmanned by illness, and his mental excitement fast becoming intolerable, when he heard a low strain of music, from the Swedenborgian chapel, hard by. Its first impression was one of solemnity and rest, and its first sense, in his mind, was of relief. Perhaps it was the music of an evening meeting; or it might be that the organist and choir had met for practice. Whatever its purpose, it breathed through his heated fancy like a cool and fragrant wind. It was vague and sweet and wandering at first, straying on into a strain more mysterious and melancholy, but very shadowy and subdued, and evoking the innocent and tender moods of early youth before worldliness had hardened around his heart. Gradually, as he listened to it, the fires in his brain were allayed, and all yielded to a sense of coolness and repose. He seemed to sink from trance to trance of utter rest, and yet was dimly aware that either something in his own condition, or some supernatural accession of tone, was changing the music from its proper quality to a harmony more infinite and awful. It was still low and indeterminate and sweet, but had unaccountably and strangely swelled into a gentle and sombre dirge, incommunicably mournful, and filled with a dark significance that touched him in his depth of rest with a secret tremor and awe. As he listened, rapt and vaguely wondering, the sense of his tranced sinking seemed to come to an end, and with the feeling of one who had been descending for many hours, and at length lay motionless at the bottom of a deep, dark chasm, he heard the music fail and cease.

A pause, and then it rose again, blended with the solemn voices of the choir, sublimed and dilated now, reaching him as though from weird night gulfs of the upper air, and charged with an overmastering pathos as of the lamentations of angels. In the dimness and silence, in the aroused and exalted condition of his being, the strains seemed unearthly in their immense and desolate grandeur of sorrow, and their mournful and dark significance was now for him. Working within him the impression of vast, innumerable fleeing shadows, thick-crowding memories of all the ways and deeds of an existence fallen from its early dreams and aims, poured across the midnight of his soul, and under the streaming melancholy of the dirge, his life showed like some monstrous treason. It did not terrify or madden him; he listened to it rapt utterly as in some deadening ether of dream; yet feeling to his inmost core all its powerful grief and accusation, and quietly aghast at the sinister consciousness it gave him. Still it swelled, gathering and sounding on into yet mightier pathos, till all at once it darkened and spread wide in wild despair, and aspiring again into a pealing agony of supplication, quivered and died away in a low and funereal sigh.

The tears streamed suddenly upon his face; his soul lightened and turned dark within him; and, as one faints away, so consciousness swooned, and he fell suddenly down a precipice of sleep. The music rose again, a pensive and holy chant, and sounded on to its close, unaffected by the action of his brain, for he slept and heard it no more. He lay tranquilly, hardly seeming to breathe, in motionless repose. The room was dim and silent, and the furniture took uncouth shapes around him. The red glow upon the ceiling, from the screened fire, showed the misty figure of the phantom kneeling by his side. All light had gone from the spectral form. It knelt beside him, mutely, as in prayer. Once it gazed at his quiet face with a mournful tenderness, and its shadowy hands caressed his forehead. Then it resumed its former attitude, and the slow hours crept by.

At last it rose and glided to the table, on which lay the open letter. It seemed to try to lift the sheets with its misty hands, but vainly. Next it essayed the lifting of a pen which lay there, but failed. It was a piteous sight, to see its idle efforts on these shapes of grosser matter, which appeared now to have to it but the existence of illusions. Wandering about the shadowy room, it wrung its phantom hands as in despair.

Presently it grew still. Then it passed quickly to his side, and stood before him. He slept calmly. It placed one ghostly hand above his forehead, and with the other pointed to the open letter. In this attitude its shape grew momentarily more distinct. It began to kindle into brightness. The pale flame again flowed from its hand, streaming downward to his brain. A look of trouble darkened the sleeping face. Stronger,—stronger; brighter,—brighter; until, at last, it stood before him, a glorious shape of light, with an awful look of commanding love in its shining features: and the sleeper sprang to his feet with a cry!

The phantom had vanished. He saw nothing. His first impression was, not that he had dreamed, but that, awaking in the familiar room, he had seen the spirit of his dead friend, bright and awful by his side, and that it had gone! In the flash of that quick change, from sleeping to waking, he had detected, he thought, the unearthly being that, he now felt, watched him from behind the air, and it had vanished! The library was the same as in the moment of that supernatural revealing; the open letter lay upon the table still; only that was gone which had made these common aspects terrible. Then all the hard, strong scepticism of his nature, which had been driven backward by the shock of his first conviction, recoiled, and rushed within him, violently struggling for its former vantage-ground; till, at length, it achieved the foothold for a doubt. Could he have dreamed? The ghost, invisible, still watched him. Yes, a dream,— only a dream; but, how vivid, how strange! With a slow thrill creeping through his veins, the blood curdling at his heart, a cold sweat starting on his forehead, he stared through the dimness of the room. All was vacancy.

With a strong shudder, he strode forward, and turned up the flames of the chandelier. A flood of garish light filled the apartment. In a moment, remembering the letter to which the phantom of his dream had pointed, he turned and took it from the table. The last page lay upward, and every word of the solemn counsel at the end seemed to dilate on the paper, and all its mighty meaning rushed upon his soul. Trembling in his own despite, he laid it down and moved away. A physician, he remembered that he was in a state of violent nervous excitement, and thought that when he grew calmer its effects would pass from him. But the hand that had touched him had gone down deeper than the physician, and reached what God had made.

He strove in vain. The very room, in its light and silence, and the lurking sentiment of something watching him, became terrible. He could not endure it. The devils in his heart, grown pusillanimous, cowered beneath the flashing strokes of his aroused and terrible conscience. He could not endure it. He must go out. He will walk the streets. It is not late,—it is but ten o'clock. He will go.

The air of his dream still hung heavily about him. He was in the street,—he hardly remembered how he had got there, or when; but there he was, wrapped up from the searching cold, thinking, with a quiet horror in his mind, of the darkened room he had left behind, and haunted by the sense that something was groping about there in the darkness, searching for him. The night was still and cold. The full moon was in the zenith. Its icy splendor lay on the bare streets, and on the walls of the dwellings. The lighted oblong squares of curtained windows, here and there, seemed dim and waxen in the frigid glory. The familiar aspect of the quarter had passed away, leaving behind only a corpse-like neighborhood, whose huge, dead features, staring rigidly through the thin, white shroud of moonlight that covered all, left no breath upon the stainless skies. Through the vast silence of the night he passed along; the very sound of his footfalls was remote to his muffled sense.

Gradually, as he reached the first corner, he had an uneasy feeling that a thing—a formless, unimaginable thing—was dogging him. He had thought of going down to his club-room; but he now shrank from entering, with this thing near him, the lighted rooms where his set were busy with cards and billiards, over their liquors and cigars, and where the heated air was full of their idle faces and careless chatter, lest some one should bawl out that he was pale, and ask him what was the matter, and he should answer, tremblingly, that something was following him, and was near him then! He must get rid of it first; he must walk quickly, and baffle its pursuit by turning sharp corners, and plunging into devious streets and crooked lanes, and so lose it!

It was difficult to reach through memory to the crazy chaos of his mind on that night, and recall the route he took while haunted by this feeling; but he afterward remembered that, without any other purpose than to baffle his imaginary pursuer, he traversed at a rapid pace a large portion of the moonlit city; always (he knew not why) avoiding the more populous thoroughfares, and choosing unfrequented and tortuous byways, but never ridding himself of that horrible confusion of mind in which the faces of his dead friend and the pale woman were strangely blended, nor of the fancy that he was followed. Once, as he passed the hospital where Feval died, a faint hint seemed to flash and vanish from the clouds of his lunacy, and almost identify the dogging goblin with the figure of his dream; but the conception instantly mixed with a disconnected remembrance that this was Christmas eve, and then slipped from him, and was lost. He did not pause there, but strode on. But just there, what had been frightful became hideous. For at once he was possessed with the conviction that the thing that lurked at a distance behind him was quickening its movement, and coming up to seize him. The dreadful fancy stung him like a goad, and, with a start, he accelerated his flight, horribly conscious that what he feared was slinking along in the shadow, close to the dark bulks of the houses, resolutely pursuing, and bent on overtaking him. Faster! His footfalls rang hollowly and loud on the moonlit pavement, and in contrast with their rapid thuds he felt it as something peculiarly terrible that the furtive thing behind slunk after him with soundless feet. Faster, faster! Traversing only the most unfrequented streets, and at that late hour of a cold winter night he met no one, and with a terrifying consciousness that his pursuer was gaining on him, he desperately strode on. He did not dare to look behind, dreading less what he might see than the momentary loss of speed the action might occasion. Faster, faster, faster! And all at once he knew that the dogging thing had dropped its stealthy pace and was racing up to him. With a bound he broke into a run, seeing, hearing, heeding nothing, aware only that the other was silently louping on his track two steps to his one; and with that frantic apprehension upon him, he gained the next street, flung himself around the corner with his back to the wall, and his arms convulsively drawn up for a grapple; and felt something rush whirring past his flank, striking him on the shoulder as it went by, with a buffet that made a shock break through his frame. That shock restored him to his senses. His delusion was suddenly shattered. The goblin was gone. He was free.

He stood panting, like one just roused from some terrible dream, wiping the reeking perspiration from his forehead, and thinking confusedly and wearily what a fool he had been. He felt he had wandered a long distance from his house, but had no distinct perception of his whereabouts. He only knew he was in some thinly peopled street, whose familiar aspect seemed lost to him in the magical disguise the superb moonlight had thrown over all. Suddenly a film seemed to drop from his eyes, as they became riveted on a lighted window, on the opposite side of the way. He started, and a secret terror crept over him, vaguely mixed with the memory of the shock he had felt as he turned the last corner, and his distinct, awful feeling that something invisible had passed him. At the same instant he felt, and thrilled to feel, a touch, as of a light finger, on his cheek. He was in Hanover Street. Before him was the house,—the oyster-room staring at him through the lighted transparencies of its two windows, like two square eyes, below; and his tenant's light in a chamber above! The added shock which this discovery gave to the heaving of his heart made him gasp for breath. Could it be? Did he still dream? While he stood panting and staring at the building the city clocks began to strike. Eleven o'clock; it was ten when he came away; how he must have driven! His thoughts caught up the word. Driven,—by what? Driven from his house in horror, through street and lane, over half the city,—driven,—hunted in terror, and smitten by a shock here! Driven,—driven! He could not rid his mind of the word, nor of the meaning it suggested. The pavements about him began to ring and echo with the tramp of many feet, and the cold, brittle air was shivered with the noisy voices that had roared and bawled applause and laughter at the National Theatre all the evening, and were now singing and howling homeward. Groups of rude men, and ruder boys, their breaths steaming in the icy air, began to tramp by, jostling him as they passed, till he was forced to draw back to the wall, and give them the sidewalk. Dazed and giddy, in cold fear, and with the returning sense of something near him, he stood and watched the groups that pushed and tumbled in through the entrance of the oyster-room, whistling and chattering as they went, and banging the door behind them. He noticed that some came out presently, banging the door harder, and went, smoking and shouting, down the street. Still they poured in and out, while the street was startled with their stimulated riot, and the bar-room within echoed their trampling feet and hoarse voices. Then, as his glance wandered upward to his tenant's window, he thought of the sick child, mixing this hideous discord in the dreams of fever. The word brought up the name and the thought of his dead friend. "In the name of the Saviour, I charge you be true and tender to mankind!" The memory of these words seemed to ring clearly, as if a voice had spoken them, above the roar that suddenly rose in his mind. In that moment he felt himself a wretched and most guilty man. He felt that his cruel words had entered that humble home, to make desperate poverty more desperate, to sicken sickness, and to sadden sorrow. Before him was the dram-shop, let and licensed to nourish the worst and most brutal appetites and instincts of human natures, at the sacrifice of all their highest and holiest tendencies. The throng of tipplers and drunkards was swarming through its hopeless door, to gulp the fiery liquor whose fumes give all shames, vices, miseries, and crimes a lawless strength and life, and change the man into the pig or tiger. Murder was done, or nearly done, within those walls last night. Within those walls no good was ever done; but daily, unmitigated evil, whose results were reaching on to torture unborn generations. He had consented to it all! He could not falter, or equivocate, or evade, or excuse. His dead friend's words rang in his conscience like the trump of the judgment angel. He was conquered.

Slowly, the resolve instantly to go in uprose within him, and with it a change came upon his spirit, and the natural world, sadder than before, but sweeter, seemed to come back to him. A great feeling of relief flowed upon his mind. Pale and trembling still, he crossed the street with a quick, unsteady step, entered a yard at the side of the house, and, brushing by a host of white, rattling spectres of frozen clothes, which dangled from lines in the enclosure, mounted some wooden steps, and rang the bell. In a minute he heard footsteps within, and saw the gleam of a lamp. His heart palpitated violently as he heard the lock turning, lest the answerer of his summons might be his tenant. The door opened, and, to his relief, he stood before a rather decent-looking Irishman, bending forward in his stocking-feet, with one boot and a lamp in his hand. The man stared at him from a wild head of tumbled red hair, with a half-smile round his loose open mouth, and said, "Begorra!" This was a second-floor tenant.

Dr. Renton was relieved at the sight of him; but he rather failed in an attempt at his rent-day suavity of manner, when he said,—

"Good evening, Mr. Flanagan. Do you think I can see Mrs. Miller to-night?"

"She's up there, docther, anyway." Mr. Flanagan made a sudden start for the stairs, with the boot and lamp at arm's length before him, and stopped as suddenly. "Yull go up? or wud she come down to ye?" There was as much anxious indecision in Mr. Flanagan's general aspect, pending the reply, as if he had to answer the question himself.

"I'll go up, Mr. Flanagan," returned Dr. Renton, stepping in, after a pause, and shutting the door. "But I'm afraid she's in bed."

"Naw—she's not, sur." Mr. Flanagan made another feint with the boot and lamp at the stairs, but stopped again in curious bewilderment, and rubbed his head. Then, with another inspiration, and speaking with such velocity that his words ran into each other, pell-mell, he continued: "Th' small girl's sick, sur. Begorra, I wor just pullin' on th' boots tuh gaw for the docther, in th' nixt streth, an' summons him to her relehf, fur it's bad she is. A'id betther be goan." Another start, and a movement to put on the boot instantly, baffled by his getting the lamp into the leg of it, and involving himself in difficulties in trying to get it out again without dropping either, and stopped finally by Dr. Renton.

27

"You needn't go, Mr. Flanagan. I'll see to the child. Don't go."

He stepped slowly up the stairs, followed by the bewildered Flanagan. All this time Dr. Renton was listening to the racket from the bar-room. Clinking of glasses, rattling of dishes, trampling of feet, oaths and laughter, and a confused din of coarse voices, mingling with boisterous calls for oysters and drink, came, hardly deadened by the partition walls, from the haunt below, and echoed through the corridors. Loud enough within,—louder in the street without, where the oysters and drink were reeling and roaring off to brutal dreams. People trying to sleep here; a sick child up stairs. Listen! "Two stew! One roast! Four ale! Hurry 'em up! Three stew! In number six! One fancy—two roast! One sling! Three brandy—hot! Two stew! One whisk' skin! Hurry 'em up! What yeh 'bout! Three brand' punch—hot! Four stew! What-ye-e-h 'BOUT! Two gin-cock-t'il! One stew! Hu-r-r-y 'em up!" Clashing, rattling, cursing, swearing, laughing, shouting, trampling, stumbling, driving, slamming of doors. "Hu-r-ry 'em up."

"Flanagan," said Dr. Renton, stopping at the first landing, "do you have this noise every night?"

"Naise? Hoo! Divil a night, docther, but I'm wehked out ov me bed wid 'em, Sundays an' all. Sure didn't they murdher wan of 'em, out an' out, last night!"

"Is the man dead?"

"Dead? Troth he is. An' cowld."

"H'm"—through his compressed lips. "Flanagan, you needn't come up. I know the door. Just hold the light for me here. There, that'll do. Thank you." He whispered the last words from the top of the second flight.

"Are ye there, docther?" Flanagan anxious to the last, and trying to peer up at him with the lamplight in his eyes.

"Yes. That'll do. Thank you!" in the same whisper. Before he could tap at the door, then darkening in the receding light, it opened suddenly, and a big Irish-woman bounced out, and then whisked in again, calling to some one in an inner room, "Here he is, Mrs. Mill'r"; and then bounced out again, with a, "Walk royt in, if you plaze; here's the choild"; and whisked in again, with a "Sure an'

28

Jehms was quick"; never once looking at him, and utterly unconscious of the presence of her landlord. He had hardly stepped into the room and taken off his hat, when Mrs. Miller came from the inner chamber with a lamp in her hand. How she started! With her pale face grown suddenly paler, and her hand on her bosom, she could only exclaim, "Why, it's Dr. Renton!" and stand, still and dumb, gazing with a frightened look at his face, whiter than her own. Whereupon Mrs. Flanagan came bolting out again, with wild eyes and a sort of stupefied horror in her good, coarse, Irish features; and then, with some uncouth ejaculation, ran back, and was heard to tumble over something within, and tumble something else over in her fall, and gather herself up with a subdued howl, and subside.

"Mrs. Miller," began Dr. Renton, in a low, husky voice, glancing at her frightened face, "I hope you'll be composed. I spoke to you very harshly and rudely to-night; but I really was not myself—I was in anger—and I ask your pardon. Please to overlook it all, and—but I will speak of this presently; now—I am a physician; will you let me look now at your sick child?"

He spoke hurriedly, but with evident sincerity. For a moment her lips faltered; then a slow flush came up, with a quick change of expression on her thin, worn face, and, reddening to painful scarlet, died away in a deeper pallor.

"Dr. Renton," she said, hastily, "I have no ill-feeling for you, sir, and I know you were hurt and vexed; and I know you have tried to make it up to me again, sir, secretly. I know who it was, now; but I can't take it, sir. You must take it back. You know it was you sent it, sir?"

"Mrs. Miller," he replied, puzzled beyond measure, "I don't understand you. What do you mean?"

"Don't deny it, sir. Please not to," she said imploringly, the tears starting to her eyes. "I am very grateful,—indeed I am. But I can't accept it. Do take it again."

"Mrs. Miller," he replied, in a hasty voice, "what do you mean? I have sent you nothing,—nothing at all. I have, therefore, nothing to receive again."

She looked at him fixedly, evidently impressed by the fervor of his denial.

"You sent me nothing to-night, sir?" she asked, doubtfully.

"Nothing at any time, nothing," he answered, firmly.

It would have been folly to have disbelieved the truthful look of his wondering face, and she turned away in amazement and confusion. There was a long pause.

"I hope, Mrs. Miller, you will not refuse any assistance I can render to your child," he said, at length.

She started, and replied, tremblingly and confusedly, "No, sir; we shall be grateful to you, if you can save her"; and went quickly, with a strange abstraction on her white face, into the inner room. He followed her at once, and, hardly glancing at Mrs. Flanagan, who sat there in stupefaction, with her apron over her head and face, he laid his hat on a table, went to the bedside of the little girl, and felt her head and pulse. He soon satisfied himself that the little sufferer was in no danger, under proper remedies, and now dashed down a prescription on a leaf from his pocket-book. Mrs. Flanagan, who had come out from the retirement of her apron, to stare stupidly at him during the examination, suddenly bobbed up on her legs, with enlightened alacrity, when he asked if there was any one that could go out to the apothecary's, and said, "Sure I wull!" He had a little trouble to make her understand that the prescription, which she took by the corner, holding it away from her, as if it were going to explode presently, and staring at it upside down, was to be left— "left, mind you, Mrs. Flanagan—with the apothecary—Mr. Flint—at the nearest corner—and he will give you some things, which you are to bring here." But she had shuffled off at last with a confident, "Yis, sur—aw, I knoo," her head nodding satisfied assent, and her big thumb covering the note on the margin, "Charge to Dr. C. Renton, Bowdoin Street," (which, I know, could not keep it from the eyes of the angels!) and he sat down to await her return.

"Mrs. Miller," he said, kindly, "don't be alarmed about your child. She is doing well; and, after you have given her the medicine Mrs. Flanagan will bring, you'll find her much better, to-morrow. She must be kept cool and quiet, you know, and she'll be all right soon."

"O Dr. Renton, I am very grateful," was the tremulous reply; "and we will follow all directions, sir. It is hard to keep her quiet, sir; we keep as still as we can, and the other children are very still; but the street is very noisy all the daytime and evening, sir, and—"

"I know it, Mrs. Miller. And I'm afraid those people down stairs disturb you somewhat."

"They make some stir in the evening, sir; and it's rather loud in the street sometimes, at night. The folks on the lower floors are troubled a good deal, they say."

Well they may be. Listen to the bawling outside, now, cold as it is. Hark! A hoarse group on the opposite sidewalk beginning a song,— "Ro-o-l on, sil-ver mo-o-n—" The silver moon ceases to roll in a sudden explosion of yells and laughter, sending up broken fragments of curses, ribald jeers, whoopings, and cat-calls, high into the night air. "Ga-l-a-ng! Hi-hi! What ye-e-h 'bout!"

"This is outrageous, Mrs. Miller. Where's the watchman?"

She smiled faintly. "He takes one of them off occasionally, sir; but he's afraid; they beat him sometimes." A long pause.

"Isn't your room rather cold, Mrs. Miller?" He glanced at the black stove, dimly seen in the outer room. "It is necessary to keep the rooms cool just now, but this air seems to me cold."

Receiving no answer, he looked at her, and saw the sad truth in her averted face.

"I beg your pardon," he said quickly, flushing to the roots of his hair. "I might have known, after what you said to me this evening."

"We had a little fire here to-day, sir," she said, struggling with the pride and shame of poverty; "but we have been out of firing for two or three days, and we owe the wharfman something now. The two boys picked up a few chips; but the poor children find it hard to get them, sir. Times are very hard with us, sir; indeed they are. We'd have got along better, if my husband's money had come, and your rent would have been paid—"

"Never mind the rent!—don't speak of that!" he broke in, with his face all aglow. "Mrs. Miller, I haven't done right by you,—I know it. Be frank with me. Are you in want of—have you—need of—food?"

No need of answer to that faintly stammered question. The thin, rigid face was covered from his sight by the worn, wan hands, and all the pride and shame of poverty, and all the frigid truth of cold, hunger, anxiety, and sickened sorrow they had concealed, had given

31

way at last in a rush of tears. He could not speak. With a smitten heart, he knew it all now. Ah! Dr. Renton, you know these people's tricks? you know their lying blazon of poverty, to gather sympathy?

"Mrs. Miller,"—she had ceased weeping, and as he spoke, she looked at him, with the tear-stains still on her agitated face, half ashamed that he had seen her,—"Mrs. Miller, I am sorry. This shall be remedied. Don't tell me it sha'n't! Don't! I say it shall! Mrs. Miller, I'm—I'm ashamed of myself. I am indeed."

"I am very grateful, sir, I'm sure," said she; "but we don't like to take charity, though we need help; but we can get along now, sir; for I suppose I must keep it, as you say you didn't send it, and use it for the children's sake, and thank God for his good mercy,—since I don't know, and never shall, where it came from, now."

"Mrs. Miller," he said quickly, "you spoke in this way before; and I don't know what you refer to. What do you mean by—it?"

"Oh! I forgot, sir: it puzzles me so. You see, sir, I was sitting here after I got home from your house, thinking what I should do, when Mrs. Flanagan came up stairs with a letter for me, that she said a strange man left at the door for Mrs. Miller; and Mrs. Flanagan couldn't describe him well, or understandingly; and it had no direction at all, only the man inquired who was the landlord, and if Mrs. Miller had a sick child, and then said the letter was for me; and there was no writing inside the letter, but there was fifty dollars. That's all, sir. It gave me a great shock, sir; and I couldn't think who sent it, only when you came to-night, I thought it was you; but you said it wasn't, and I never shall know who it was, now. It seems as if the hand of God was in it, sir, for it came when everything was darkest, and I was in despair."

"Why, Mrs. Miller," he slowly answered, "this is very mysterious. The man inquired if I was the owner of the house—oh! no—he only inquired who was—but then he knew I was the—oh! bother! I'm getting nowhere. Let's see. Why, it must be some one you know, or that knows your circumstances."

"But there's no one knows them but yourself; and I told you," she replied; "no one else but the people in the house. It must have been some rich person, for the letter was a gilt-edge sheet, and there was perfume in it, sir."

"Strange," he murmured. "Well, I give it up. All is, I advise you to keep it, and I'm very glad some one did his duty by you in your hour of need, though I'm sorry it was not myself. Here's Mrs. Flanagan."

There was a good deal done, and a great burden lifted off an humble heart—nay, two!—before Dr. Renton thought of going home. There was a patient gained, likely to do Dr. Renton more good than any patient he had lost. There was a kettle singing on the stove, and blowing off a happier steam than any engine ever blew on that railroad whose unmarketable stock had singed Dr. Renton's fingers. There was a yellow gleam flickering from the blazing fire on the sober binding of a good old Book upon a shelf with others, a rarer medical work than ever slipped at auction from Dr. Renton's hands, since it kept the sacred lore of Him who healed the sick, and fed the hungry, and comforted the poor, and who was also the Physician of souls.

And there were other offices performed, of lesser range than these, before he rose to go. There were cooling mixtures blended for the sick child; medicines arranged; directions given; and all the items of her tendance orderly foreseen, and put in pigeon-holes of When and How, for service.

At last he rose to go. "And now, Mrs. Miller," he said, "I'll come here at ten in the morning, and see to our patient. She'll be nicely by that time. And (listen to those brutes in the street!—twelve o'clock, too— ah! there's the bell), as I was saying, my offence to you being occasioned by your debt to me, I feel my receipt for your debt should commence my reparation to you; and I'll bring it to-morrow. Mrs. Miller, you don't quite come at me—what I mean is—you owe me, under a notice to quit, three months' rent. Consider that paid in full. I never will take a cent of it from you,—not a copper. And I take back the notice. Stay in my house as long as you like; the longer the better. But, up to this date, your rent's paid. There. I hope you'll have as happy a Christmas as circumstances will allow, and I mean you shall."

A flush of astonishment, of indefinable emotion, overspread her face.

"Dr. Renton, stop, sir!" He was moving to the door. "Please, sir, do hear me! You are very good—but I can't allow you to—Dr. Renton, we are able to pay you the rent, and we will, and we must—here— now. O, sir, my gratefulness will never fail to you—but here—here— be fair with me, sir, and do take it."

She had hurried to a chest of drawers, and came back with the letter which she had rustled apart with eager, trembling hands, and now, unfolding the single banknote it had contained, she thrust it into his fingers as they closed.

"Here, Mrs. Miller,"—she had drawn back with her arms locked on her bosom, and he stepped forward,—"no, no. This sha'n't be. Come, come, you must take it back. Good heavens!" He spoke low, but his eyes blazed in the red glow which broke out on his face, and the crisp note in his extended hand shook violently at her. "Sooner than take this money from you, I would perish in the street! What! Do you think I will rob you of the gift sent you by some one who had a human heart for the distresses I was aggravating? Sooner than— Here, take it! O my God! what's this?"

The red glow on his face went out, with this exclamation, in a pallor like marble, and he jerked back the note to his starting eyes. Globe Bank—Boston—Fifty Dollars. For a minute he gazed at the motionless bill in his hand. Then, with his hueless lips compressed, he seized the blank letter from his astonished tenant, and looked at it, turning it over and over. Grained letter-paper—gilt-edged—with a favorite perfume in it. Where's Mrs. Flanagan? Outside the door, sitting on the top of the stairs, with her apron over her head, crying. Mrs. Flanagan! Here! In she tumbled, her big feet kicking her skirts before her, and her eyes and face as red as a beet.

"Mrs. Flanagan, what kind of a looking man gave you this letter at the door to-night?"

"A-w, Docther Rinton, dawn't ax me!—Bother, an' all, an' sure an' I cudn't see him wud his fur-r hat, an' he a-ll boondled oop wud his co-at oop on his e-ars, an' his big han'kershuf smotherin' thuh mouth uv him, an' sorra a bit uv him tuh be looked at, sehvin' thuh poomple on thuh ind uv his naws."

"The what on the end of his nose?"

"Thuh poomple, sur."

"What does she mean, Mrs. Miller?" said the puzzled questioner, turning to his tenant.

"I don't know, sir, indeed," was the reply. "She said that to me, and I couldn't understand her."

"It's thuh poomple, docther. Dawn't ye knoo? Thuh big, flehmin poomple oop there." She indicated the locality, by flattening the rude tip of her own nose with her broad forefinger.

"Oh! the pimple! I have it." So he had. Netty, Netty!

He said nothing, but sat down in a chair, with his bold, white brow knitted, and the warm tears in his dark eyes.

"You know who sent it, sir, don't you?" asked his wondering tenant, catching the meaning of all this.

"Mrs. Miller, I do. But I cannot tell you. Take it, now, and use it. It is doubly yours. There. Thank you."

She had taken it with an emotion in her face that gave a quicker motion to his throbbing heart. He rose to his feet, hat in hand, and turned away. The noise of a passing group of roysterers in the street without came strangely loud into the silence of that room.

"Good night, Mrs. Miller. I'll be here in the morning. Good night."

"Good night, sir. God bless you, sir!"

He turned around quickly. The warm tears in his dark eyes had flowed on his face, which was pale; and his firm lip quivered.

"I hope He will, Mrs. Miller,—I hope He will. It should have been said oftener."

He was on the outer threshold. Mrs. Flanagan had, somehow, got there before him, with a lamp, and he followed her down through the dancing shadows, with blurred eyes. On the lower landing he stopped to hear the jar of some noisy wrangle, thick with oaths, from the bar-room. He listened for a moment, and then turned to the staring stupor of Mrs. Flanagan's rugged visage.

"Sure, they're at ut, docther, wud a wull," she said, smiling.

"Yes. Mrs. Flanagan, you'll stay up with Mrs. Miller to-night, won't you?"

"Dade an' I wull, sur."

"That's right. Do. And make her try and sleep, for she must be tired.

Keep up a fire,—not too warm, you understand. There'll be wood and coal coming to-morrow, and she'll pay you back."

"A-w, docther, dawn't noo!"

"Well, well. And—look here; have you got anything to eat in the house? Yes; well, take it up stairs. Wake up those two boys, and give them something to eat. Don't let Mrs. Miller stop you. Make her eat something. Tell her I said she must. And, first of all, get your bonnet, and go to that apothecary's,—Flint's,—for a bottle of port wine, for Mrs. Miller. Hold on. There's the order." (He had a leaf out of his pocket-book in a minute, and wrote it down.) "Go with this the first thing. Ring Flint's bell, and he'll wake up. And here's something for your own Christmas dinner, to-morrow." Out of the roll of bills he drew one of the tens—Globe Bank—Boston—and gave it to Mrs. Flanagan.

"A-w, dawn't noo, docther."

"Bother! It's for yourself, mind. Take it. There. And now unlock the door. That's it. Good night, Mrs. Flanagan."

"An' meh thuh Hawly Vurgin hape bless'n's on ye, Docther Rinton, wud a-ll thuh compliments uv thuh sehzin, for yur thuh—"

He lost the end of Mrs. Flanagan's parting benedictions in the moonlit street. He did not pause till he was at the door of the oyster-room. He paused then, to make way for a tipsy company of four, who reeled out,—the gaslight from the bar-room on the edges of their sodden, distorted faces,—giving three shouts and a yell, as they slammed the door behind them.

He pushed after a party that was just entering. They went at once for a drink to the upper end of the room, where a rowdy crew, with cigars in their mouths, and liquor in their hands, stood before the bar, in a knotty wrangle concerning some one who was killed. Where is the keeper? O, there he is, mixing hot brandy punch for two! Here, you, sir, go up quietly, and tell Mr. Rollins Dr. Renton wants to see him. The waiter came back presently to say Mr. Rollins would be right along. Twenty-five minutes past twelve. Oyster trade nearly over. Gaudy-curtained booths on the left all empty but two. Oyster-openers and waiters—three of them in all—nearly done for the night, and two of them sparring and scuffling behind a pile of oysters on the trough, with the colored print of the great prize fight between Tom Hyer and Yankee Sullivan, in a veneered frame above

36

them on the wall. Blower up from the fire opposite the bar, and stewpans and griddles empty and idle on the bench beside it, among the unwashed bowls and dishes. Oyster trade nearly over. Bar still busy.

Here comes Rollins in his shirt-sleeves, with an apron on. Thick-set, muscular man,—frizzled head, low forehead, sharp, black eyes, flabby face, with a false, greasy smile on it now, oiling over a curious, stealthy expression of mingled surprise and inquiry, as he sees his landlord here at this unusual hour.

"Come in here, Mr. Rollins; I want to speak to you."

"Yes, sir. Jim" (to the waiter), "go and tend bar." They sat down in one of the booths, and lowered the curtain. Dr. Renton, at one side of the table within, looking at Rollins, sitting leaning on his folded arms, at the other side.

"Mr. Rollins, I am told the man who was stabbed here last night is dead. Is that so?"

"Well, he is, Dr. Renton. Died this afternoon."

"Mr. Rollins, this is a serious matter; what are you going to do about it?"

"Can't help it, sir. Who's a-goin' to touch me? Called in a watchman. Whole mess of 'em had cut. Who knows 'em? Nobody knows 'em. Man that was stuck never see the fellers as stuck him in all his life till then. Didn't know which one of 'em did it. Didn't know nothing. Don't now, an' never will, 'nless he meets 'em in hell. That's all. Feller's dead, an' who's a-goin' to touch me? Can't do it. Ca-n-'t do it."

"Mr. Rollins," said Dr. Renton, thoroughly disgusted with this man's brutal indifference, "your lease expires in three days."

"Well, it does. Hope to make a renewal with you, Dr. Renton. Trade's good here. Shouldn't mind more rent on, if you insist,—hope you won't,—if it's anything in reason. Promise sollum, I sha' n't have no more fightin' in here. Couldn't help this. Accidents will happen, yo' know."

"Mr. Rollins, the case is this: if you didn't sell liquor here, you'd have no murder done in your place,—murder, sir. That man was murdered. It's your fault, and it's mine, too. I ought not to have let you the place for your business. It is a cursed traffic, and you and I ought to have found it out long ago. I have. I hope you will. Now, I advise you, as a friend, to give up selling rum for the future; you see what it comes to,—don't you? At any rate, I will not be responsible for the outrages that are perpetrated in my building any more,—I will not have liquor sold here. I refuse to renew your lease. In three days you must move."

"Dr. Renton, you hurt my feelin's. Now, how would you—"

"Mr. Rollins, I have spoken to you as a friend, and you have no cause for pain. You must quit these premises when your lease expires. I'm sorry I can't make you go before that. Make no appeals to me, if you please. I am fixed. Now, sir, good night."

The curtain was pulled up, and Rollins rolled over to his beloved bar, soothing his lacerated feelings by swearing like a pirate, while Dr. Renton strode to the door, and went into the street, homeward.

He walked fast through the magical moonlight, with a strange feeling of sternness, and tenderness, and weariness, in his mind. In this mood, the sensation of spiritual and physical fatigue gaining on him, but a quiet moonlight in all his reveries, he reached his house. He was just putting his latch-key in the door, when it was opened by James, who stared at him for a second, and then dropped his eyes, and put his hand before his nose. Dr. Renton compressed his lips on an involuntary smile.

"Ah! James, you're up late. It's near one."

"I sat up for Mrs. Renton and the young lady, sir. They're just come, and gone up stairs."

"All right, James. Take your lamp and come in here. I've got something to say to you." The man followed him into the library at once, with some wonder on his sleepy face.

"First, put some coal on that fire, and light the chandelier. I shall not go up stairs to-night." The man obeyed. "Now, James, sit down in that chair." He did so, beginning to look frightened at Dr. Renton's grave manner.

"James,"—a long pause,—"I want you to tell me the truth. Where did you go to-night? Come, I have found you out. Speak."

38

The man turned as white as a sheet, and looked wretched with the whites of his bulging eyes, and the great pimple on his nose awfully distinct in the livid hue of his features. He was a rather slavish fellow, and thought he was going to lose his situation. Please not to blame him, for he, too, was one of the poor.

"O Dr. Renton, excuse me, sir; I didn't mean doing any harm."

"James, my daughter gave you an undirected letter this evening; you carried it to one of my houses in Hanover Street. Is that true?"

"Ye-yes, sir. I couldn't help it. I only did what she told me, sir."

"James, if my daughter told you to set fire to this house, what would you do?"

"I wouldn't do it, sir," he stammered, after some hesitation.

"You wouldn't? James, if my daughter ever tells you to set fire to this house, do it, sir! Do it. At once. Do whatever she tells you. Promptly. And I'll back you."

The man stared wildly at him, as he received this astonishing command. Dr. Renton was perfectly grave, and had spoken slowly and seriously. The man was at his wits' end.

"You'll do it, James,—will you?"

"Ye-yes, sir, certainly."

"That's right. James, you're a good fellow. James, you've got a wife and children, hav'n't you?"

"Yes, sir, I have; living in the country, sir. In Chelsea, over the ferry. For cheapness, sir."

"For cheapness, eh? Hard times, James? How is it?"

"Pretty hard, sir. Close, but toler'ble comfortable. Rub and go, sir."

"Rub and go. Ve-r-y well. Rub and go. James, I'm going to raise your wages—to-morrow. Generally, because you're a good servant. Principally, because you carried that letter to-night, when my daughter asked you. I sha'n't forget it. To-morrow, mind. And if I can do anything for you, James, at any time, just tell me. That's all. Now, you'd better go to bed. And a happy Christmas to you!"

39

"Much obliged to you, sir. Same to you and many of 'em. Good night, sir." And with Dr. Renton's "good-night" he stole up to bed, thoroughly happy, and determined to obey Miss Renton's future instructions to the letter. The shower of golden light which had been raining for the last two hours had fallen even on him. It would fall all day to-morrow in many places, and the day after, and for long years to come. Would that it could broaden and increase to a general deluge, and submerge the world!

Now the whole house was still, and its master was weary. He sat there, quietly musing, feeling the sweet and tranquil presence near him. Now the fire was screened, the lights were out, save one dim glimmer, and he had lain down on the couch with the letter in his hand, and slept the dreamless sleep of a child.

He slept until the gray dawn of Christmas day stole into the room, and showed him the figure of his friend, a shape of glorious light, standing by his side, and gazing at him with large and tender eyes! He had no fear. All was deep, serene, and happy with the happiness of heaven. Looking up into that beautiful, wan face,—so tranquil,— so radiant; watching, with a childlike awe, the star-fire in those shadowy eyes; smiling faintly, with a great, unutterable love thrilling slowly through his frame, in answer to the smile of light that shone upon the phantom countenance; so he passed a space of time which seemed a calm eternity, till, at last, the communion of spirit with spirit—of mortal love with love immortal—was perfected, and the shining hands were laid on his forehead, as with a touch of air. Then the phantom smiled, and, as its shining hands were withdrawn, the thought of his daughter mingled in the vision. She was bending over him! The dawn, the room, were the same. But the ghost of Feval had gone out from earth, away to its own land!

"Father, dear father! Your eyes were open, and they did not look at me. There is a light on your face, and your features are changed! What is it,—what have you seen?"

"Hush, darling: here—kneel by me, for a little while, and be still. I have seen the dead."

She knelt by him, burying her awe-struck face in his bosom, and clung to him with all the fervor of her soul. He clasped her to his breast, and for minutes all was still.

"Dear child, good and dear child!"

The voice was tremulous and low. She lifted her fair, bright countenance, now convulsed with a secret trouble, and dimmed with streaming tears, to his, and gazed on him. His eyes were shining; but his pallid cheeks, like hers, were wet with tears. How still the room was! How like a thought of solemn tenderness the pale gray dawn! The world was far away, and his soul still wandered in the peaceful awe of his dream. The world was coming back to him,—but oh! how changed!—in the trouble of his daughter's face.

"Darling, what is it? Why are you here? Why are you weeping? Dear child, the friend of my better days,—of the boyhood when I had noble aims, and life was beautiful before me,—he has been here! I have seen him. He has been with me—oh! for a good I cannot tell!"

"Father, dear father!"—he had risen, and sat upon the couch, but she still knelt before him, weeping, and clasped his hands in hers,— "I thought of you and of this letter, all the time. All last night till I slept, and then I dreamed you were tearing it to pieces, and trampling on it. I awoke, and lay thinking of you, and of ——. And I thought I heard you come down stairs, and I came here to find you. But you were lying here so quietly, with your eyes open, and so strange a light on your face. And I knew,—I knew you were dreaming of him, and that you saw him, for the letter lay beside you. O father! forgive me, but do hear me! In the name of this day,—it's Christmas day, father,—in the name of the time when we must both die,—in the name of that time, father, hear me! That poor woman last night,—O father! forgive me, but don't tear that letter in pieces and trample it under foot! You know what I mean—you know—you know. Don't tear it, and tread it under foot."

She clung to him, sobbing violently, her face buried in his hands.

"Hush, hush! It's all well,—it's all well. Here, sit by me. So. I have—" His voice failed him, and he paused. But sitting by him,—clinging to him,—her face hidden in his bosom,—she heard the strong beating of his disenchanted heart.

"My child, I know your meaning. I will not tear the letter to pieces and trample it under foot. God forgive me my life's slight to those words. But I learned their value last night, in the house where your blank letter had entered before me."

She started, and looked into his face steadfastly, while a bright scarlet shot into her own.

41

"I know all, Netty,—all. Your secret was well kept, but it is yours and mine now. It was well done, darling, well done. O, I have been through strange mysteries of thought and life since that starving woman sat here! Well—thank God!"

"Father, what have you done?" The flush had failed, but a glad color still brightened her face, while the tears stood trembling in her eyes.

"All that you wished yesterday," he answered. "And all that you ever could have wished, henceforth I will do."

"O father!" She stopped. The bright scarlet shot again into her face, but with an April shower of tears, and the rainbow of a smile.

"Listen to me, Netty, and I will tell you, and only you, what I have done." Then, while she mutely listened, sitting by his side, and the dawn of Christmas broadened into Christmas day, he told her all.

And when he had told all, and emotion was stilled, they sat together in silence for a time, she with her innocent head drooped upon his shoulder, and her eyes closed, lost in tender and mystic reveries; and he musing with a contrite heart. Till at last, the stir of daily life began to waken in the quiet dwelling, and without, from steeples in the frosty air, there was a sound of bells.

They rose silently, and stood, clinging to each other, side by side.

"Love, we must part," he said, gravely and tenderly. "Read me, before we go, the closing lines of George Feval's letter. In the spirit of this let me strive to live. Let it be for me the lesson of the day. Let it also be the lesson of my life."

Her face was pale and lit with exaltation as she took the letter from his hand. There was a pause, and then upon the thrilling and tender silver of her voice, the words arose like solemn music:—

"Farewell—farewell! But, oh! take my counsel into memory on Christmas Day, and forever. Once again, the ancient prophecy of peace and good-will shines on a world of wars and wrongs and woes. Its soft ray shines into the darkness of a land wherein swarm slaves, poor laborers, social pariahs, weeping women, homeless exiles, hunted fugitives, despised aliens, drunkards, convicts, wicked children, and Magdalens unredeemed. These are but the ghastliest figures in that sad army of humanity which advances, by a dreadful road, to the Golden Age of the poets' dream. These are your

42

sisters and your brothers. Love them all. Beware of wronging one of them by word or deed. O friend! strong in wealth for so much good,—take my last counsel. In the name of the Saviour, I charge you, be true and tender to mankind. Come out from Babylon into manhood, and live and labor for the fallen, the neglected, the suffering, and the poor. Lover of arts, customs, laws, institutions, and forms of society, love these things only as they help mankind! With stern love, overturn them, or help to overturn them, when they become cruel to a single—the humblest—human being. In the world's scale, social position, influence, public power, the applause of majorities, heaps of funded gold, services rendered to creeds, codes, sects, parties, or federations—they weigh weight; but in God's scale—remember!—on the day if hope, remember!—your least service to Humanity outweighs them all."

THE FOUR-FIFTEEN EXPRESS

BY AMELIA B. EDWARDS

I

T he events which I am about to relate took place between nine and ten years ago. Sebastopol had fallen in the early spring; the peace of Paris had been concluded since March; our commercial relations with the Russian Empire were but recently renewed; and I, returning home after my first northward journey since the war, was well pleased with the prospect of spending the month of December under the hospitable and thoroughly English roof of my excellent friend Jonathan Jelf, Esquire, of Dumbleton Manor, Clayborough, East Anglia. Travelling in the interests of the well-known firm in which it is my lot to be a junior partner, I had been called upon to visit not only the capitals of Russia and Poland, but had found it also necessary to pass some weeks among the trading-ports of the Baltic; whence it came that the year was already far spent before I again set foot on English soil, and that, instead of shooting pheasants with him, as I had hoped, in October, I came to be my friend's guest during the more genial Christmastide.

My voyage over, and a few days given up to business in Liverpool and London, I hastened down to Clayborough with all the delight of a school-boy whose holidays are at hand. My way lay by the Great East Anglian line as far as Clayborough station, where I was to be met by one of the Dumbleton carriages and conveyed across the remaining nine miles of country. It was a foggy afternoon, singularly warm for the 4th of December, and I had arranged to leave London by the 4.15 express. The early darkness of winter had already closed in; the lamps were lighted in the carriages; a clinging damp dimmed the windows, adhered to the door-handles, and pervaded all the atmosphere; while the gas-jets at the neighboring bookstand diffused a luminous haze that only served to make the gloom of the terminus more visible. Having arrived some seven minutes before the starting of the train, and, by the connivance of the guard, taken sole possession of an empty compartment, I lighted my travelling-

44

lamp, made myself particularly snug, and settled down to the undisturbed enjoyment of a book and a cigar. Great, therefore, was my disappointment when, at the last moment, a gentleman came hurrying along the platform, glanced into my carriage, opened the locked door with a private key, and stepped in.

It struck me at the first glance that I had seen him before,—a tall, spare man, thin-lipped, light-eyed, with an ungraceful stoop in the shoulders, and scant gray hair worn somewhat long upon the collar. He carried a light water-proof coat, an umbrella, and a large brown japanned deed-box, which last he placed under the seat. This done, he felt carefully in his breast-pocket, as if to make certain of the safety of his purse or pocket-book; laid his umbrella in the netting overhead; spread the water-proof across his knees; and exchanged his hat for a travelling-cap of some Scotch material. By this time the train was moving out of the station, and into the faint gray of the wintry twilight beyond.

I now recognized my companion. I recognized him from the moment when he removed his hat and uncovered the lofty, furrowed, and somewhat narrow brow beneath. I had met him, as I distinctly remembered, some three years before, at the very house for which, in all probability, he was now bound, like myself. His name was Dwerrihouse; he was a lawyer by profession; and, if I was not greatly mistaken, was first-cousin to the wife of my host. I knew also that he was a man eminently "well to do," both as regarded his professional and private means. The Jelfs entertained him with that sort of observant courtesy which falls to the lot of the rich relation; the children made much of him; and the old butler, albeit somewhat surly "to the general," treated him with deference. I thought, observing him by the vague mixture of lamplight and twilight, that Mrs. Jelf's cousin looked all the worse for the three years' wear and tear which had gone over his head since our last meeting. He was very pale, and had a restless light in his eye that I did not remember to have observed before. The anxious lines, too, about his mouth were deepened, and there was a cavernous, hollow look about his cheeks and temples which seemed to speak of sickness or sorrow. He had glanced at me as he came in, but without any gleam of recognition in his face. Now he glanced again, as I fancied, somewhat doubtfully. When he did so for the third or fourth time, I ventured to address him.

"Mr. John Dwerrihouse, I think?"

"That is my name," he replied.

"I had the pleasure of meeting you at Dumbleton about three years ago."

Mr. Dwerrihouse bowed.

"I thought I knew your face," he said. "But your name, I regret to say—"

"Langford,—William Langford. I have known Jonathan Jelf since we were boys together at Merchant Taylor's, and I generally spend a few weeks at Dumbleton in the shooting-season. I suppose we are bound for the same destination?"

"Not if you are on your way to the Manor," he replied. "I am travelling upon business,—rather troublesome business, too,— whilst you, doubtless, have only pleasure in view."

"Just so. I am in the habit of looking forward to this visit as to the brightest three weeks in all the year."

"It is a pleasant house," said Mr. Dwerrihouse.

"The pleasantest I know."

"And Jelf is thoroughly hospitable."

"The best and kindest fellow in the world!"

"They have invited me to spend Christmas week with them," pursued Mr. Dwerrihouse, after a moment's pause.

"And you are coming?"

"I cannot tell. It must depend on the issue of this business which I have in hand. You have heard, perhaps, that we are about to construct a branch line from Blackwater to Stockbridge."

I explained that I had been for some months away from England, and had therefore heard nothing of the contemplated improvement.

Mr. Dwerrihouse smiled complacently.

"It will be an improvement," he said; "a great improvement. Stockbridge is a flourishing town, and needs but a more direct

46

railway communication with the metropolis to become an important centre of commerce. This branch was my own idea. I brought the project before the board, and have myself superintended the execution of it up to the present time."

"You are an East Anglian director, I presume?"

"My interest in the company," replied Mr. Dwerrihouse, "is threefold. I am a director; I am a considerable shareholder; and, as head of the firm of Dwerrihouse, Dwerrihouse, and Craik, I am the company's principal solicitor."

Loquacious, self-important, full of his pet project, and apparently unable to talk on any other subject, Mr. Dwerrihouse then went on to tell of the opposition he had encountered and the obstacles he had overcome in the cause of the Stockbridge branch. I was entertained with a multitude of local details and local grievances. The rapacity of one squire; the impracticability of another; the indignation of the rector whose glebe was threatened; the culpable indifference of the Stockbridge townspeople, who could not be brought to see that their most vital interests hinged upon a junction with the Great East Anglian line; the spite of the local newspaper; and the unheard-of difficulties attending the Common question,— were each and all laid before me with a circumstantiality that possessed the deepest interest for my excellent fellow-traveller, but none whatever for myself. From these, to my despair, he went on to more intricate matters: to the approximate expenses of construction per mile; to the estimates sent in by different contractors; to the probable traffic returns of the new line; to the provisional clauses of the new Act as enumerated in Schedule D of the company's last half-yearly report; and so on, and on, and on, till my head ached, and my attention flagged, and my eyes kept closing in spite of every effort that I made to keep them open. At length I was roused by these words:—

"Seventy-five thousand pounds, cash down."

"Seventy-five thousand pounds, cash down," I repeated, in the liveliest tone I could assume. "That is a heavy sum."

"A heavy sum to carry here," replied Mr. Dwerrihouse, pointing significantly to his breast-pocket; "but a mere fraction of what we shall ultimately have to pay."

"You do not mean to say that you have seventy-five thousand pounds at this moment upon your person?" I exclaimed.

"My good sir, have I not been telling you so for the last half-hour?" said Mr. Dwerrihouse, testily.

"That money has to be paid over at half past eight o'clock this evening, at the office of Sir Thomas's solicitors, on completion of the deed of sale."

"But how will you get across by night from Blackwater to Stockbridge with seventy-five thousand pounds in your pocket?"

"To Stockbridge!" echoed the lawyer. "I find I have made myself very imperfectly understood. I thought I had explained how this sum only carries us as far as Mallingford,—the first stage, as it were, of our journey,—and how our route from Blackwater to Mallingford lies entirely through Sir Thomas Liddell's property."

"I beg your pardon," I stammered. "I fear my thoughts were wandering. So you only go as far as Mallingford to-night?"

"Precisely. I shall get a conveyance from the 'Blackwater Arms.' And you?"

"O, Jelf sends a trap to meet me at Clayborough! Can I be the bearer of any message from you?"

"You may say, if you please, Mr. Langford, that I wished I could have been your companion all the way, and that I will come over, if possible, before Christmas."

"Nothing more?"

Mr. Dwerrihouse smiled grimly. "Well," he said, "you may tell my cousin that she need not burn the hall down in my honor this time, and that I shall be obliged if she will order the blue-room chimney to be swept before I arrive."

"That sounds tragic. Had you a conflagration on the occasion of your last visit to Dumbleton?"

"Something like it. There had been no fire lighted in my bedroom since the spring, the flue was foul, and the rooks had built in it; so when I went up to dress for dinner, I found the room full of smoke, and the chimney on fire. Are we already at Blackwater?"

The train had gradually come to a pause while Mr. Dwerrihouse was speaking, and, on putting my head out of the window, I could see the station some few hundred yards ahead. There was another train before us blocking the way, and the guard was making use of the delay to collect the Blackwater tickets. I had scarcely ascertained our position, when the ruddy-faced official appeared at our carriage-door.

"Tickets, sir!" said he.

"I am for Clayborough," I replied, holding out the tiny pink card.

He took it; glanced at it by the light of his little lantern; gave it back; looked, as I fancied, somewhat sharply at my fellow-traveller, and disappeared.

"He did not ask for yours," I said with some surprise.

"They never do," replied Mr. Dwerrihouse. "They all know me; and, of course, I travel free."

"Blackwater! Blackwater!" cried the porter, running along the platform beside us, as we glided into the station.

Mr. Dwerrihouse pulled out his deed-box, put his travelling-cap in his pocket, resumed his hat, took down his umbrella, and prepared to be gone.

"Many thanks, Mr. Langford, for your society," he said, with old-fashioned courtesy. "I wish you a good evening."

"Good evening," I replied, putting out my hand.

But he either did not see it, or did not choose to see it, and, slightly lifting his hat, stepped out upon the platform. Having done this, he moved slowly away, and mingled with the departing crowd.

Leaning forward to watch him out of sight, I trod upon something which proved to be a cigar-case. It had fallen, no doubt, from the pocket of his water-proof coat, and was made of dark morocco leather, with a silver monogram upon the side. I sprang out of the carriage just as the guard came up to lock me in.

"Is there one minute to spare?" I asked eagerly. "The gentleman who travelled down with me from town has dropped his cigar-case; he is not yet out of the station!"

"Just a minute and a half, sir," replied the guard. "You must be quick."

I dashed along the platform as fast as my feet could carry me. It was a large station, and Mr. Dwerrihouse had by this time got more than half-way to the farther end.

I, however, saw him distinctly, moving slowly with the stream. Then, as I drew nearer, I saw that he had met some friend,—that they were talking as they walked,—that they presently fell back somewhat from the crowd, and stood aside in earnest conversation. I made straight for the spot where they were waiting. There was a vivid gas-jet just above their heads, and the light fell full upon their faces. I saw both distinctly,—the face of Mr. Dwerrihouse and the face of his companion. Running, breathless, eager as I was, getting in the way of porters and passengers, and fearful every instant lest I should see the train going on without me, I yet observed that the new-comer was considerably younger and shorter than the director, that he was sandy-haired, mustachioed, small-featured, and dressed in a close-cut suit of Scotch tweed. I was now within a few yards of them. I ran against a stout gentleman,—I was nearly knocked down by a luggage-truck,—I stumbled over a carpet-bag,—I gained the spot just as the driver's whistle warned me to return.

To my utter stupefaction they were no longer there. I had seen them but two seconds before,—and they were gone! I stood still. I looked to right and left. I saw no sign of them in any direction. It was as if the platform had gaped and swallowed them.

"There were two gentlemen standing here a moment ago," I said to a porter at my elbow; "which way can they have gone?"

"I saw no gentlemen, sir," replied the man.

The whistle shrilled out again. The guard, far up the platform, held up his arm, and shouted to me to "Come on!"

"If you're going on by this train, sir," said the porter, "you must run for it."

I did run for it, just gained the carriage as the train began to move, was shoved in by the guard, and left breathless and bewildered, with Mr. Dwerrihouse's cigar-case still in my hand.

It was the strangest disappearance in the world. It was like a transformation trick in a pantomime. They were there one moment,—palpably there, talking, with the gaslight full upon their faces; and the next moment they were gone. There was no door near,—no window,—no staircase. It was a mere slip of barren platform, tapestried with big advertisements. Could anything be more mysterious?

It was not worth thinking about; and yet, for my life, I could not help pondering upon it,—pondering, wondering, conjecturing, turning it over and over in my mind, and beating my brains for a solution of the enigma. I thought of it all the way from Blackwater to Clayborough. I thought of it all the way from Clayborough to Dumbleton, as I rattled along the smooth highway in a trim dog-cart drawn by a splendid black mare, and driven by the silentest and dapperest of East Anglian grooms.

We did the nine miles in something less than an hour, and pulled up before the lodge-gates just as the church-clock was striking half past seven. A couple of minutes more, and the warm glow of the lighted hall was flooding out upon the gravel, a hearty grasp was on my hand, and a clear jovial voice was bidding me "Welcome to Dumbleton."

"And now, my dear fellow," said my host, when the first greeting was over, "you have no time to spare. We dine at eight, and there are people coming to meet you; so you must just get the dressing business over as quickly as may be. By the way, you will meet some acquaintances. The Biddulphs are coming, and Prendergast (Prendergast, of the Skirmishers) is staying in the house. Adieu! Mrs. Jelf will be expecting you in the drawing-room."

I was ushered to my room,—not the blue room, of which Mr. Dwerrihouse had made disagreeable experience, but a pretty little bachelor's chamber, hung with a delicate chintz, and made cheerful by a blazing fire. I unlocked my portmanteau. I tried to be expeditious; but the memory of my railway adventure haunted me. I could not get free of it. I could not shake it off. It impeded me,—it worried me,—it tripped me up,—it caused me to mislay my studs,—to mistie my cravat,—to wrench the buttons off my gloves. Worst of all, it made me so late that the party had all assembled before I reached the drawing-room. I had scarcely paid my respects to Mrs. Jelf when dinner was announced, and we paired off, some eight or ten couples strong, into the dining-room.

I am not going to describe either the guests or the dinner. All provincial parties bear the strictest family resemblance, and I am not aware that an East Anglian banquet offers any exception to the rule. There was the usual country baronet and his wife; there were the usual country parsons and their wives; there was the sempiternal turkey and haunch of venison. Vanitas vanitatum. There is nothing new under the sun.

I was placed about midway down the table. I had taken one rector's wife down to dinner, and I had another at my left hand. They talked across me, and their talk was about babies. It was dreadfully dull. At length there came a pause. The entrées had just been removed, and the turkey had come upon the scene. The conversation had all along been of the languidest, but at this moment it happened to have stagnated altogether. Jelf was carving the turkey. Mrs. Jelf looked as if she was trying to think of something to say. Everybody else was silent. Moved by an unlucky impulse, I thought I would relate my adventure.

"By the way, Jelf," I began, "I came down part of the way to-day with a friend of yours."

"Indeed!" said the master of the feast, slicing scientifically into the breast of the turkey. "With whom, pray?"

"With one who bade me tell you that he should, if possible, pay you a visit before Christmas."

"I cannot think who that could be," said my friend, smiling.

"It must be Major Thorp," suggested Mrs. Jelf.

I shook my head.

"It was not Major Thorp," I replied. "It was a near relation of your own, Mrs. Jelf."

"Then I am more puzzled than ever," replied my hostess. "Pray tell me who it was."

"It was no less a person than your cousin, Mr. John Dwerrihouse."

Jonathan Jelf laid down his knife and fork. Mrs. Jelf looked at me in a strange, startled way, and said never a word.

"And he desired me to tell you, my dear madam, that you need not

52

take the trouble to burn the hall down in his honor this time; but only to have the chimney of the blue room swept before his arrival."

Before I had reached the end of my sentence, I became aware of something ominous in the faces of the guests. I felt I had said something which I had better have left unsaid, and that for some unexplained reason my words had evoked a general consternation. I sat confounded, not daring to utter another syllable, and for at least two whole minutes there was dead silence round the table. Then Captain Prendergast came to the rescue.

"You have been abroad for some months, have you not, Mr. Langford?" he said, with the desperation of one who flings himself into the breach. "I heard you had been to Russia. Surely you have something to tell us of the state and temper of the country after the war?"

I was heartily grateful to the gallant Skirmisher for this diversion in my favor. I answered him, I fear, somewhat lamely; but he kept the conversation up, and presently one or two others joined in, and so the difficulty, whatever it might have been, was bridged over. Bridged over, but not repaired. A something, an awkwardness, a visible constraint, remained. The guests hitherto had been simply dull; but now they were evidently uncomfortable and embarrassed.

The dessert had scarcely been placed upon the table when the ladies left the room. I seized the opportunity to select a vacant chair next Captain Prendergast.

"In Heaven's name," I whispered, "what was the matter just now? What had I said?"

"You mentioned the name of John Dwerrihouse."

"What of that? I had seen him not two hours before."

"It is a most astounding circumstance that you should have seen him," said Captain Prendergast. "Are you sure it was he?"

"As sure as of my own identity. We were talking all the way between London and Blackwater. But why does that surprise you?"

"Because," replied Captain Prendergast, dropping his voice to the lowest whisper,—"because John Dwerrihouse absconded three months ago, with seventy-five thousand pounds of the company's money, and has never been heard of since."

53

II

John Dwerrihouse had absconded three months ago,—and I had seen him only a few hours back. John Dwerrihouse had embezzled seventy-five thousand pounds of the company's money, yet told me that he carried that sum upon his person. Were ever facts so strangely incongruous, so difficult to reconcile? How should he have ventured again into the light of day? How dared he show himself along the line? Above all, what had he been doing throughout those mysterious three months of disappearance?

Perplexing questions these. Questions which at once suggested themselves to the minds of all concerned, but which admitted of no easy solution. I could find no reply to them. Captain Prendergast had not even a suggestion to offer. Jonathan Jelf, who seized the first opportunity of drawing me aside and learning all that I had to tell, was more amazed and bewildered than either of us. He came to my room that night, when all the guests were gone, and we talked the thing over from every point of view; without, it must be confessed, arriving at any kind of conclusion.

"I do not ask you," he said, "whether you can have mistaken your man. That is impossible."

"As impossible as that I should mistake some stranger for yourself."

"It is not a question of looks or voice, but of facts. That he should have alluded to the fire in the blue room is proof enough of John Dwerrihouse's identity. How did he look?"

"Older, I thought. Considerably older, paler, and more anxious."

"He has had enough to make him look anxious, anyhow," said my friend, gloomily; "be he innocent or guilty."

"I am inclined to believe that he is innocent," I replied. "He showed no embarrassment when I addressed him, and no uneasiness when the guard came round. His conversation was open to a fault. I might almost say that he talked too freely of the business which he had in hand."

"That again is strange; for I know no one more reticent on such

54

subjects. He actually told you that he had the seventy-five thousand pounds in his pocket?"

"He did."

"Humph! My wife has an idea about it, and she may be right—"

"What idea?"

"Well, she fancies,—women are so clever, you know, at putting themselves inside people's motives,—she fancies that he was tempted; that he did actually take the money; and that he has been concealing himself these three months in some wild part of the country,—struggling possibly with his conscience all the time, and daring neither to abscond with his booty nor to come back and restore it."

"But now that he has come back?"

"That is the point. She conceives that he has probably thrown himself upon the company's mercy; made restitution of the money; and, being forgiven, is permitted to carry the business through as if nothing whatever had happened."

"The last," I replied, "is an impossible case. Mrs. Jelf thinks like a generous and delicate-minded woman, but not in the least like a board of railway directors. They would never carry forgiveness so far."

"I fear not; and yet it is the only conjecture that bears a semblance of likelihood. However, we can run over to Clayborough to-morrow, and see if anything is to be learned. By the way, Prendergast tells me you picked up his cigar-case."

"I did so, and here it is."

Jelf took the cigar-case, examined it by the light of the lamp, and said at once that it was beyond doubt Mr. Dwerrihouse's property, and that he remembered to have seen him use it.

"Here, too, is his monogram on the side," he added. "A big J transfixing a capital D. He used to carry the same on his note-paper."

"It offers, at all events, a proof that I was not dreaming."

"Ay; but it is time you were asleep and dreaming now. I am ashamed to have kept you up so long. Good night."

"Good night, and remember that I am more than ready to go with you to Clayborough, or Blackwater, or London, or anywhere, if I can be of the least service."

"Thanks! I know you mean it, old friend, and it may be that I shall put you to the test. Once more, good night."

So we parted for that night, and met again in the breakfast-room at half past eight next morning. It was a hurried, silent, uncomfortable meal. None of us had slept well, and all were thinking of the same subject. Mrs. Jelf had evidently been crying; Jelf was impatient to be off; and both Captain Prendergast and myself felt ourselves to be in the painful position of outsiders, who are involuntarily brought into a domestic trouble. Within twenty minutes after we had left the breakfast-table the dog-cart was brought round, and my friend and I were on the road to Clayborough.

"Tell you what it is, Langford," he said, as we sped along between the wintry hedges, "I do not much fancy to bring up Dwerrihouse's name at Clayborough. All the officials know that he is my wife's relation, and the subject just now is hardly a pleasant one. If you don't much mind, we will take the 11.10 to Blackwater. It's an important station, and we shall stand a far better chance of picking up information there than at Clayborough."

So we took the 11.10, which happened to be an express, and, arriving at Blackwater about a quarter before twelve, proceeded at once to prosecute our inquiry.

We began by asking for the station-master,—a big, blunt, business-like person, who at once averred that he knew Mr. John Dwerrihouse perfectly well, and that there was no director on the line whom he had seen and spoken to so frequently.

"He used to be down here two or three times a week, about three months ago," said he, "when the new line was first set afoot; but since then, you know, gentlemen—"

He paused, significantly.

Jelf flushed scarlet.

56

"Yes, yes," he said hurriedly, "we know all about that. The point now to be ascertained is whether anything has been seen or heard of him lately."

"Not to my knowledge," replied the station-master.

"He is not known to have been down the line any time yesterday, for instance?"

The station-master shook his head.

"The East Anglian, sir," said he, "is about the last place where he would dare to show himself. Why, there isn't a station-master, there isn't a guard, there isn't a porter, who doesn't know Mr. Dwerrihouse by sight as well as he knows his own face in the looking-glass; or who wouldn't telegraph for the police as soon as he had set eyes on him at any point along the line. Bless you, sir! there's been a standing order out against him ever since the twenty-fifth of September last."

"And yet," pursued my friend, "a gentleman who travelled down yesterday from London to Clayborough by the afternoon express testifies that he saw Mr. Dwerrihouse in the train, and that Mr. Dwerrihouse alighted at Blackwater station."

"Quite impossible, sir," replied the station-master, promptly.

"Why impossible?"

"Because there is no station along the line where he is so well known, or where he would run so great a risk. It would be just running his head into the lion's mouth. He would have been mad to come nigh Blackwater station; and if he had come, he would have been arrested before he left the platform."

"Can you tell me who took the Blackwater tickets of that train?"

"I can, sir. It was the guard,—Benjamin Somers."

"And where can I find him?"

"You can find him, sir, by staying here, if you please, till one o'clock. He will be coming through with the up express from Crampton, which stays at Blackwater for ten minutes."

We waited for the up express, beguiling the time as best we could by strolling along the Blackwater road till we came almost to the outskirts of the town, from which the station was distant nearly a couple of miles. By one o'clock we were back again upon the platform, and waiting for the train. It came punctually, and I at once recognized the ruddy-faced guard who had gone down with my train the evening before.

"The gentlemen want to ask you something about Mr. Dwerrihouse, Somers," said the station-master, by way of introduction.

The guard flashed a keen glance from my face to Jelf's, and back again to mine.

"Mr. John Dwerrihouse, the late director?" said he, interrogatively.

"The same," replied my friend. "Should you know him if you saw him?"

"Anywhere, sir."

"Do you know if he was in the 4.15 express yesterday afternoon?"

"He was not, sir."

"How can you answer so positively?"

"Because I looked into every carriage, and saw every face in that train, and I could take my oath that Mr. Dwerrihouse was not in it. This gentleman was," he added, turning sharply upon me. "I don't know that I ever saw him before in my life, but I remember his face perfectly. You nearly missed taking your seat in time at this station, sir, and you got out at Clayborough."

"Quite true, guard," I replied; "but do you not also remember the face of the gentleman who travelled down in the same carriage with me as far as here?"

"It was my impression, sir, that you travelled down alone," said Somers, with a look of some surprise.

"By no means. I had a fellow-traveller as far as Blackwater, and it was in trying to restore him the cigar-case which he had dropped in the carriage that I so nearly let you go on without me."

"I remember your saying something about a cigar-case, certainly," replied the guard, "but—"

58

"You asked for my ticket just before we entered the station."

"I did, sir."

"Then you must have seen him. He sat in the corner next the very door to which you came."

"No, indeed. I saw no one."

I looked at Jelf. I began to think the guard was in the ex-director's confidence, and paid for his silence.

"If I had seen another traveller I should have asked for his ticket," added Somers. "Did you see me ask for his ticket, sir?"

"I observed that you did not ask for it, but he explained that by saying—" I hesitated. I feared I might be telling too much, and so broke off abruptly.

The guard and the station-master exchanged glances. The former looked impatiently at his watch.

"I am obliged to go on in four minutes more, sir," he said.

"One last question, then," interposed Jelf, with a sort of desperation. "If this gentleman's fellow-traveller had been Mr. John Dwerrihouse, and he had been sitting in the corner next the door by which you took the tickets, could you have failed to see and recognize him?"

"No, sir; it would have been quite impossible."

"And you are certain you did not see him?"

"As I said before, sir, I could take my oath I did not see him. And if it wasn't that I don't like to contradict a gentleman, I would say I could also take my oath that this gentleman was quite alone in the carriage the whole way from London to Clayborough. Why, sir," he added, dropping his voice so as to be inaudible to the station-master, who had been called away to speak to some person close by, "you expressly asked me to give you a compartment to yourself, and I did so. I locked you in, and you were so good as to give me something for myself."

"Yes; but Mr. Dwerrihouse had a key of his own."

59

"I never saw him, sir; I saw no one in that compartment but yourself. Beg pardon, sir, my time's up."

And with this the ruddy guard touched his cap and was gone. In another minute the heavy panting of the engine began afresh, and the train glided slowly out of the station.

We looked at each other for some moments in silence. I was the first to speak.

"Mr. Benjamin Somers knows more than he chooses to tell," I said.

"Humph! do you think so?"

"It must be. He could not have come to the door without seeing him. It's impossible."

"There is one thing not impossible, my dear fellow."

"What is that?"

"That you may have fallen asleep, and dreamt the whole thing."

"Could I dream of a branch line that I had never heard of? Could I dream of a hundred and one business details that had no kind of interest for me? Could I dream of the seventy-five thousand pounds?"

"Perhaps you might have seen or heard some vague account of the affair while you were abroad. It might have made no impression upon you at the time, and might have come back to you in your dreams,—recalled, perhaps, by the mere names of the stations on the line."

"What about the fire in the chimney of the blue room,—should I have heard of that during my journey?"

"Well, no; I admit there is a difficulty about that point."

"And what about the cigar-case?"

"Ay, by Jove! there is the cigar-case. That is a stubborn fact. Well, it's a mysterious affair, and it will need a better detective than myself, I fancy, to clear it up. I suppose we may as well go home."

III

A week had not gone by when I received a letter from the Secretary of the East Anglian Railway Company, requesting the favor of my attendance at a special board meeting, not then many days distant. No reasons were alleged, and no apologies offered, for this demand upon my time; but they had heard, it was clear, of my inquiries anent the missing director, and had a mind to put me through some sort of official examination upon the subject. Being still a guest at Dumbleton Hall, I had to go up to London for the purpose, and Jonathan Jelf accompanied me. I found the direction of the Great East Anglian line represented by a party of some twelve or fourteen gentlemen seated in solemn conclave round a huge green-baize table, in a gloomy board-room, adjoining the London terminus.

Being courteously received by the chairman (who at once began by saying that certain statements of mine respecting Mr. John Dwerrihouse had come to the knowledge of the direction, and that they in consequence desired to confer with me on those points), we were placed at the table, and the inquiry proceeded in due form.

I was first asked if I knew Mr. John Dwerrihouse, how long I had been acquainted with him, and whether I could identify him at sight. I was then asked when I had seen him last. To which I replied, "On the fourth of this present month, December, eighteen hundred and fifty-six." Then came the inquiry of where I had seen him on that fourth day of December; to which I replied that I met him in a first-class compartment of the 4.15 down express; that he got in just as the train was leaving the London terminus, and that he alighted at Blackwater station. The chairman then inquired whether I had held any communication with my fellow-traveller; whereupon I related, as nearly as I could remember it, the whole bulk and substance of Mr. John Dwerrihouse's diffuse information respecting the new branch line.

To all this the board listened with profound attention, while the chairman presided and the secretary took notes. I then produced the cigar-case. It was passed from hand to hand, and recognized by all. There was not a man present who did not remember that plain cigar-case with its silver monogram, or to whom it seemed anything less than entirely corroborative of my evidence. When at length I had told all that I had to tell, the chairman whispered something to the secretary; the secretary touched a silver hand-bell; and the guard, Benjamin Somers, was ushered into the room. He was then examined as carefully as myself. He declared that he knew Mr. John Dwerrihouse perfectly well; that he could not be mistaken in him; that he remembered going down with the 4.15 express on the afternoon in question; that he remembered me; and that, there being one or two empty first-class compartments on that especial afternoon, he had, in compliance with my request, placed me in a carriage by myself. He was positive that I remained alone in that compartment all the way from London to Clayborough. He was ready to take his oath that Mr. Dwerrihouse was neither in that carriage with me, nor in any compartment of that train. He remembered distinctly to have examined my ticket at Blackwater; was certain that there was no one else at that time in the carriage; could not have failed to observe a second person, if there had been one; had that second person been Mr. John Dwerrihouse, should have quietly double-locked the door of the carriage, and have at once given information to the Blackwater station-master. So clear, so decisive, so ready, was Somers with this testimony, that the board looked fairly puzzled.

"You hear this person's statement, Mr. Langford," said the chairman. "It contradicts yours in every particular. What have you to say in reply?"

"I can only repeat what I said before. I am quite as positive of the truth of my own assertions as Mr. Somers can be of the truth of his."

"You say that Mr. Dwerrihouse alighted at Blackwater, and that he was in possession of a private key. Are you sure that he had not alighted by means of that key before the guard came round for the tickets?"

"I am quite positive that he did not leave the carriage till the train had fairly entered the station, and the other Blackwater passengers alighted. I even saw that he was met there by a friend."

"Indeed! Did you see that person distinctly?"

"Quite distinctly."

"Can you describe his appearance?"

"I think so. He was short and very slight, sandy-haired, with a bushy mustache and beard, and he wore a closely fitting suit of gray tweed. His age I should take to be about thirty-eight or forty."

"Did Mr. Dwerrihouse leave the station in this person's company?"

"I cannot tell. I saw them walking together down the platform, and then I saw them standing aside under a gas-jet, talking earnestly. After that I lost sight of them quite suddenly; and just then my train went on, and I with it"

The chairman and secretary conferred together in an undertone. The directors whispered to each other. One or two looked suspiciously at the guard. I could see that my evidence remained unshaken, and that, like myself, they suspected some complicity between the guard and the defaulter.

"How far did you conduct that 4.15 express on the day in question, Somers?" asked the chairman.

"All through, sir," replied the guard; "from London to Crampton."

"How was it that you were not relieved at Clayborough? I thought there was always a change of guards at Clayborough."

"There used to be, sir, till the new regulations came in force last midsummer; since when, the guards in charge of express trains go the whole way through."

The chairman turned to the secretary.

"I think it would be as well," he said, "if we had the day-book to refer to upon this point."

Again the secretary touched the silver hand-bell, and desired the porter in attendance to summon Mr. Raikes. From a word or two dropped by another of the directors, I gathered that Mr. Raikes was one of the under-secretaries.

He came,—a small, slight, sandy-haired, keen-eyed man, with an eager, nervous manner, and a forest of light beard and mustache. He just showed himself at the door of the board-room, and, being requested to bring a certain day-book from a certain shelf in a certain room, bowed and vanished.

He was there such a moment, and the surprise of seeing him was so great and sudden, that it was not till the door had closed upon him that I found voice to speak. He was no sooner gone, however, than I sprang to my feet.

"That person," I said, "is the same who met Mr. Dwerrihouse upon the platform at Blackwater!"

There was a general movement of surprise. The chairman looked grave, and somewhat agitated.

"Take care, Mr. Langford," he said, "take care what you say!"

"I am as positive of his identity as of my own."

"Do you consider the consequences of your words? Do you consider that you are bringing a charge of the gravest character against one of the company's servants?"

"I am willing to be put upon my oath, if necessary. The man who came to that door a minute since is the same whom I saw talking with Mr. Dwerrihouse on the Blackwater platform. Were he twenty times the company's servant, I could say neither more nor less."

The chairman turned again to the guard.

"Did you see Mr. Raikes in the train, or on the platform?" he asked.

Somers shook his head.

"I am confident Mr. Raikes was not in the train," he said; "and I certainly did not see him on the platform."

The chairman turned next to the secretary.

"Mr. Raikes is in your office, Mr. Hunter," he said. "Can you remember if he was absent on the fourth instant?"

"I do not think he was," replied the secretary; "but I am not prepared to speak positively. I have been away most afternoons myself lately, and Mr. Raikes might easily have absented himself if he had been disposed."

At this moment the under-secretary returned with the day-book under his arm.

"Be pleased to refer, Mr. Raikes," said the chairman, "to the entries of the fourth instant, and see what Benjamin Somers's duties were on that day."

Mr. Raikes threw open the cumbrous volume, and ran a practised eye and finger down some three or four successive columns of entries. Stopping suddenly at the foot of a page, he then read aloud that Benjamin Somers had on that day conducted the 4.15 express from London to Crampton.

The chairman leaned forward in his seat, looked the under-secretary full in the face, and said, quite sharply and suddenly,—

"Where were you, Mr. Raikes, on the same afternoon?"

"I, sir?"

"You, Mr. Raikes. Where were you on the afternoon and evening of the fourth of the present month?"

"Here, sir,—in Mr. Hunter's office. Where else should I be?"

There was a dash of trepidation in the under-secretary's voice as he said this; but his look of surprise was natural enough.

"We have some reason for believing, Mr. Raikes, that you were absent that afternoon without leave. Was this the case?"

"Certainly not, sir. I have not had a day's holiday since September. Mr. Hunter will bear me out in this."

Mr. Hunter repeated what he had previously said on the subject, but added that the clerks in the adjoining office would be certain to know. Whereupon the senior clerk, a grave, middle-aged person, in green glasses, was summoned and interrogated.

His testimony cleared the under-secretary at once. He declared that Mr. Raikes had in no instance, to his knowledge, been absent during office hours since his return from his annual holiday in September.

I was confounded. The chairman turned to me with a smile, in which a shade of covert annoyance was scarcely apparent.

"You hear, Mr. Langford?" he said.

"I hear, sir; but my conviction remains unshaken."

"I fear, Mr. Langford, that your convictions are very insufficiently based," replied the chairman, with a doubtful cough. "I fear that you 'dream dreams,' and mistake them for actual occurrences. It is a dangerous habit of mind, and might lead to dangerous results. Mr. Raikes here would have found himself in an unpleasant position, had he not proved so satisfactory an alibi."

I was about to reply, but he gave me no time.

"I think, gentlemen," he went on to say, addressing the board, "that we should be wasting time to push this inquiry further. Mr. Langford's evidence would seem to be of an equal value throughout. The testimony of Benjamin Somers disproves his first statement, and the testimony of the last witness disproves his second. I think we may conclude that Mr. Langford fell asleep in the train on the occasion of his journey to Clayborough, and dreamt an unusually vivid and circumstantial dream,—of which, however, we have now heard quite enough."

There are few things more annoying than to find one's positive convictions met with incredulity. I could not help feeling impatience at the turn that affairs had taken. I was not proof against the civil sarcasm of the chairman's manner. Most intolerable of all, however, was the quiet smile lurking about the corners of Benjamin Somers's mouth, and the half-triumphant, half-malicious gleam in the eyes of the under-secretary. The man was evidently puzzled, and somewhat alarmed. His looks seemed furtively to interrogate me. Who was I? What did I want? Why had I come there to do him an ill turn with his employers? What was it to me whether or no he was absent without leave?

Seeing all this, and perhaps more irritated by it than the thing deserved, I begged leave to detain the attention of the board for a moment longer. Jelf plucked me impatiently by the sleeve.

"Better let the thing drop," he whispered. "The chairman's right enough. You dreamt it; and the less said now the better."

I was not to be silenced, however, in this fashion. I had yet something to say, and I would say it. It was to this effect: that dreams were not usually productive of tangible results, and that I requested to know in what way the chairman conceived I had evolved from my dream so substantial and well-made a delusion as the cigar-case which I had had the honor to place before him at the commencement of our interview.

"The cigar-case, I admit, Mr. Langford," the chairman replied, "is a very strong point in your evidence. It is your only strong point, however, and there is just a possibility that we may all be misled by a mere accidental resemblance. Will you permit me to see the case again?"

"It is unlikely," I said, as I handed it to him, "that any other should bear precisely this monogram, and yet be in all other particulars exactly similar."

The chairman examined it for a moment in silence, and then passed it to Mr. Hunter. Mr. Hunter turned it over and over, and shook his head.

"This is no mere resemblance," he said. "It is John Dwerrihouse's cigar-case to a certainty. I remember it perfectly. I have seen it a hundred times."

"I believe I may say the same," added the chairman. "Yet how account for the way in which Mr. Langford asserts that it came into his possession?"

"I can only repeat," I replied, "that I found it on the floor of the carriage after Mr. Dwerrihouse had alighted. It was in leaning out to look after him that I trod upon it; and it was in running after him for the purpose of restoring it that I saw—or believed I saw—Mr. Raikes standing aside with him in earnest conversation."

Again I felt Jonathan Jelf plucking at my sleeve.

"Look at Raikes," he whispered,—"look at Raikes!"

I turned to where the under-secretary had been standing a moment before, and saw him, white as death with lips trembling and livid, stealing towards the door.

To conceive a sudden, strange, and indefinite suspicion; to fling myself in his way; to take him by the shoulders as if he were a child, and turn his craven face, perforce, towards the board, were with me the work of an instant.

"Look at him!" I exclaimed. "Look at his face! I ask no better witness to the truth of my words."

The chairman's brow darkened.

"Mr. Raikes," he said, sternly, "if you know anything, you had better speak."

Vainly trying to wrench himself from my grasp, the under-secretary stammered out an incoherent denial.

"Let me go," he said. "I know nothing,—you have no right to detain me,—let me go!"

"Did you, or did you not, meet Mr. John Dwerrihouse at Blackwater station? The charge brought against you is either true or false. If true, you will do well to throw yourself upon the mercy of the board, and make full confession of all that you know."

The under-secretary wrung his hands in an agony of helpless terror.

"I was away," he cried. "I was two hundred miles away at the time! I know nothing about it—I have nothing to confess—I am innocent—I call God to witness I am innocent!"

"Two hundred miles away!" echoed the chairman. "What do you mean?"

"I was in Devonshire. I had three weeks' leave of absence—I appeal to Mr. Hunter—Mr. Hunter knows I had three weeks' leave of absence! I was in Devonshire all the time—I can prove I was in Devonshire!"

Seeing him so abject, so incoherent, so wild with apprehension, the directors began to whisper gravely among themselves; while one got quietly up, and called the porter to guard the door.

"What has your being in Devonshire to do with the matter?" said the chairman. "When were you in Devonshire?"

"Mr. Raikes took his leave in September," said the secretary; "about the time when Mr. Dwerrihouse disappeared."

"I never even heard that he had disappeared till I came back!"

"That must remain to be proved," said the chairman. "I shall at once put this matter in the hands of the police. In the mean while, Mr. Raikes, being myself a magistrate, and used to deal with these cases, I advise you to offer no resistance, but to confess while confession may yet do you service. As for your accomplice—"

68

The frightened wretch fell upon his knees.

"I had no accomplice!" he cried. "Only have mercy upon me,—only spare my life, and I will confess all! I didn't mean to harm him! I didn't mean to hurt a hair of his head. Only have mercy upon me, and let me go!"

The chairman rose in his place, pale and agitated. "Good heavens!" he exclaimed, "what horrible mystery is this? What does it mean?"

"As sure as there is a God in heaven," said Jonathan Jelf, "it means that murder has been done."

"No—no—no!" shrieked Raikes, still upon his knees, and cowering like a beaten hound. "Not murder! No jury that ever sat could bring it in murder. I thought I had only stunned him—I never meant to do more than stun him! Manslaughter—manslaughter—not murder!"

Overcome by the horror of this unexpected revelation, the chairman covered his face with his hand, and for a moment or two remained silent.

"Miserable man," he said at length, "you have betrayed yourself."

"You bade me confess! You urged me to throw myself upon the mercy of the board!"

"You have confessed to a crime which no one suspected you of having committed," replied the chairman, "and which this board has no power either to punish or forgive. All that I can do for you is to advise you to submit to the law, to plead guilty, and to conceal nothing. When did you do this deed?"

The guilty man rose to his feet, and leaned heavily against the table. His answer came reluctantly, like the speech of one dreaming.

"On the twenty-second of September!"

On the twenty-second of September! I looked in Jonathan Jelf's face, and he in mine. I felt my own paling with a strange sense of wonder and dread. I saw his blanch suddenly, even to the lips.

"Merciful heaven!" he whispered, "what was it, then, that you saw in the train?"

What was it that I saw in the train? That question remains

69

unanswered to this day. I have never been able to reply to it. I only know that it bore the living likeness of the murdered man, whose body had then been lying some ten weeks under a rough pile of branches, and brambles, and rotting leaves, at the bottom of a deserted chalk-pit about half-way between Blackwater and Mallingford. I know that it spoke, and moved, and looked as that man spoke, and moved, and looked in life; that I heard, or seemed to hear, things related which I could never otherwise have learned; that I was guided, as it were, by that vision on the platform to the identification of the murderer; and that, a passive instrument myself, I was destined, by means of these mysterious teachings, to bring about the ends of justice. For these things I have never been able to account.

As for that matter of the cigar-case, it proved on inquiry, that the carriage in which I travelled down that afternoon to Clayborough had not been in use for several weeks, and was in point of fact the same in which poor John Dwerrihouse had performed his last journey. The case had, doubtless, been dropped by him, and had lain unnoticed till I found it.

Upon the details of the murder I have no need to dwell. Those who desire more ample particulars may find them, and the written confession of Augustus Raikes, in the files of the Times for 1856. Enough that the under-secretary, knowing the history of the new line, and following the negotiation step by step through all its stages, determined to waylay Mr. Dwerrihouse, rob him of the seventy-five thousand pounds, and escape to America with his booty.

In order to effect these ends he obtained leave of absence a few days before the time appointed for the payment of the money; secured his passage across the Atlantic in a steamer advertised to start on the twenty-third; provided himself with a heavily loaded "life-preserver," and went down to Blackwater to await the arrival of his victim. How he met him on the platform with a pretended message from the board; how he offered to conduct him by a short cut across the fields to Mallingford; how, having brought him to a lonely place, he struck him down with the life-preserver, and so killed him; and how, finding what he had done, he dragged the body to the verge of an out-of-the-way chalk-pit, and there flung it in, and piled it over with branches and brambles,—are facts still fresh in the memories of those who, like the connoisseurs in De Quincey's famous essay,

70

regard murder as a fine art. Strangely enough, the murderer, having done his work, was afraid to leave the country. He declared that he had not intended to take the director's life, but only to stun and rob him; and that, finding the blow had killed, he dared not fly for fear of drawing down suspicion upon his own head. As a mere robber he would have been safe in the States, but as a murderer he would inevitably have been pursued, and given up to justice. So he forfeited his passage, returned to the office as usual at the end of his leave, and locked up his ill-gotten thousands till a more convenient opportunity. In the mean while he had the satisfaction of finding that Mr. Dwerrihouse was universally believed to have absconded with the money, no one knew how or whither.

Whether he meant murder or not, however, Mr. Augustus Raikes paid the full penalty of his crime, and was hanged at the Old Bailey in the second week in January, 1857. Those who desire to make his further acquaintance may see him any day (admirably done in wax) in the Chamber of Horrors at Madame Tussaud's exhibition, in Baker Street. He is there to be found in the midst of a select society of ladies and gentlemen of atrocious memory, dressed in the close-cut tweed suit which he wore on the evening of the murder, and holding in his hand the identical life-preserver with which he committed it.

THE SIGNAL-MAN

BY CHARLES DICKENS

Halloa! Below there!"

When he heard a voice thus calling to him, he was standing at the door of his box, with a flag in his hand, furled round its short pole. One would have thought, considering the nature of the ground, that he could not have doubted from what quarter the voice came; but, instead of looking up to where I stood on the top of the steep cutting nearly over his head, he turned himself about and looked down the Line. There was something remarkable in his manner of doing so, though I could not have said, for my life, what. But I know it was remarkable enough to attract my notice, even though his figure was foreshortened and shadowed, down in the deep trench, and mine was high above him, and so steeped in the glow of an angry sunset that I had shaded my eyes with my hand before I saw him at all.

"Halloa! Below!"

From looking down the Line, he turned himself about again, and, raising his eyes, saw my figure high above him.

"Is there any path by which I can come down and speak to you?"

He looked up at me without replying, and I looked down at him without pressing him too soon with a repetition of my idle question. Just then there came a vague vibration in the earth and air, quickly changing into a violent pulsation, and an oncoming rush that caused me to start back, as though it had force to draw me down. When such vapor as rose to my height from this rapid train had passed me and was skimming away over the landscape, I looked down again, and saw him refurling the flag he had shown while the train went by.

I repeated my inquiry. After a pause, during which he seemed to regard me with fixed attention, he motioned with his rolled-up flag towards a point on my level, some two or three hundred yards distant. I called down to him, "All right!" and made for that point.

72

There, by dint of looking closely about me, I found a rough zigzag descending path notched out; which I followed.

The cutting was extremely deep, and unusually precipitate. It was made through a clammy stone that became oozier and wetter as I went down. For these reasons, I found the way long enough to give me time to recall a singular air of reluctance or compulsion with which he had pointed out the path.

When I came down low enough upon the zigzag descent to see him again, I saw that he was standing between the rails on the way by which the train had lately passed, in an attitude as if he were waiting for me to appear. He had his left hand at his chin, and that left elbow rested on his right hand crossed over his breast. His attitude was one of such expectation and watchfulness, that I stopped a moment, wondering at it.

I resumed my downward way, and, stepping out upon the level of the railroad and drawing nearer to him, saw that he was a dark, sallow man, with a dark beard and rather heavy eyebrows. His post was in as solitary and dismal a place as ever I saw. On either side, a dripping-wet wall of jagged stone, excluding all view but a strip of sky: the perspective one way, only a crooked prolongation of this great dungeon; the shorter perspective in the other direction, terminating in a gloomy red light, and the gloomier entrance to a black tunnel, in whose massive architecture there was a barbarous, depressing, and forbidding air. So little sunlight ever found its way to this spot, and it had an earthy deadly smell; and so much cold wind rushed through it, that it struck chill to me, as if I had left the natural world.

Before he stirred, I was near enough to him to have touched him. Not even then removing his eyes from mine, he stepped back one step, and lifted his hand.

This was a lonesome post to occupy (I said), and it had riveted my attention when I looked down from up yonder. A visitor was a rarity, I should suppose; not an unwelcome rarity, I hoped? In me, he merely saw a man who had been shut up within narrow limits all his life, and who, being at last set free, had a newly awakened interest in these great works. To such purpose I spoke to him; but I am far from sure of the terms I used, for, besides that I am not happy in opening any conversation, there was something in the man that daunted me.

He directed a most curious look towards the red light near the tunnel's mouth, and looked all about it, as if something were missing from it, and then looked at me.

That light was part of his charge? Was it not?

He answered in a low voice, "Don't you know it is?"

The monstrous thought came into my mind, as I perused the fixed eyes and the saturnine face, that this was a spirit, not a man. I have speculated since whether there may have been infection in his mind.

In my turn, I stepped back. But in making the action, I detected in his eyes some latent fear of me. This put the monstrous thought to flight.

"You look at me," I said, forcing a smile, "as if you had a dread of me."

"I was doubtful," he returned, "whether I had seen you before."

"Where?"

He pointed to the red light he had looked at.

"There?" I said.

Intently watchful of me, he replied (but without sound), "Yes."

"My good fellow, what should I do there? However, be that as it may, I never was there, you may swear."

"I think I may," he rejoined. "Yes, I am sure I may."

His manner cleared, like my own. He replied to my remarks with readiness, and in well-chosen words. Had he much to do there? Yes; that was to say, he had enough responsibility to bear; but exactness and watchfulness were what was required of him, and of actual work—manual labor—he had next to none. To change that signal, to trim those lights, and to turn this iron handle now and then, was all he had to do under that head. Regarding those many long and lonely hours of which I seemed to make so much, he could only say that the routine of his life had shaped itself into that form, and he had grown used to it. He had taught himself a language down here,—if only to know it by sight, and to have formed his own crude

74

ideas of its pronunciation, could be called learning it. He had also worked at fractions and decimals, and tried a little algebra; but he was, and had been as a boy, a poor hand at figures. Was it necessary for him, when on duty, always to remain in that channel of damp air, and could he never rise into the sunshine from between those high stone walls? Why, that depended upon times and circumstances. Under some conditions there would be less upon the Line than under others, and the same held good as to certain hours of the day and night. In bright weather, he did choose occasions for getting a little above these lower shadows; but, being at all times liable to be called by his electric bell, and at such times listening for it with redoubled anxiety, the relief was less than I would suppose.

He took me into his box, where there was a fire, a desk for an official book in which he had to make certain entries, a telegraphic instrument with its dial face and needles, and the little bell of which he had spoken. On my trusting that he would excuse the remark that he had been well educated, and (I hoped I might say without offence) perhaps educated above that station, he observed that instances of slight incongruity in such-wise would rarely be found wanting among large bodies of men; that he had heard it was so in workhouses, in the police force, even in that last desperate resource, the army; and that he knew it was so, more or less, in any great railway staff. He had been, when young (if I could believe it, sitting in that hut; he scarcely could), a student of natural philosophy, and had attended lectures; but he had run wild, misused his opportunities, gone down, and never risen again. He had no complaint to offer about that. He had made his bed, and he lay upon it. It was far too late to make another.

All that I have here condensed he said in a quiet manner, with his grave dark regards divided between me and the fire. He threw in the word "Sir" from time to time, and especially when he referred to his youth, as though to request me to understand that he claimed to be nothing but what I found him. He was several times interrupted by the little bell, and had to read off messages, and send replies. Once he had to stand without the door and display a flag as a train passed, and make some verbal communication to the driver. In the discharge of his duties I observed him to be remarkably exact and vigilant, breaking off his discourse at a syllable, and remaining silent until what he had to do was done.

In a word, I should have set this man down as one of the safest of men to be employed in that capacity, but for the circumstance that while he was speaking to me he twice broke off with a fallen color, turned his face towards the little bell when it did NOT ring, opened the door of the hut (which was kept shut to exclude the unhealthy damp), and looked out towards the red light near the mouth of the tunnel. On both of those occasions he came back to the fire with the inexplicable air upon him which I had remarked, without being able to define, when we were so far asunder.

Said I, when I rose to leave him, "You almost make me think that I have met with a contented man."

(I am afraid I must acknowledge that I said it to lead him on.)

"I believe I used to be so," he rejoined, in the low voice in which he had first spoken; "but I am troubled, sir, I am troubled."

He would have recalled the words if he could. He had said them, however, and I took them up quickly.

"With what? What is your trouble?"

"It is very difficult to impart, sir. It is very, very difficult to speak of. If ever you make me another visit, I will try to tell you."

"But I expressly intend to make you another visit. Say, when shall it be?"

"I go off early in the morning, and I shall be on again at ten to-morrow night, sir."

"I will come at eleven."

He thanked me, and went out at the door with me. "I'll show my white light, sir," he said, in his peculiar low voice, "till you have found the way up. When you have found it, don't call out! And when you are at the top, don't call out!"

His manner seemed to make the place strike colder to me, but I said no more than, "Very well."

"And when you come down to-morrow night, don't call out! Let me ask you a parting question. What made you cry, 'Halloa! Below there!' to-night?"

"Heaven knows," said I. "I cried something to that effect—"

"Not to that effect, sir. Those were the very words. I know them well."

"Admit those were the very words. I said them, no doubt, because I saw you below."

"For no other reason?"

"What other reason could I possibly have?"

"You had no feeling that they were conveyed to you in any supernatural way?"

"No."

He wished me good night, and held up his light. I walked by the side of the down Line of rails (with a very disagreeable sensation of a train coming behind me), until I found the path. It was easier to mount than to descend, and I got back to my inn without any adventure.

Punctual to my appointment, I placed my foot on the first notch of the zigzag next night, as the distant clocks were striking eleven. He was waiting for me at the bottom, with his white light on.

"I have not called out," I said, when we came close together; "may I speak now?"

"By all means, sir."

"Good night, then, and here's my hand."

"Good night, sir, and here's mine."

With that, we walked side by side to his box, entered it, closed the door, and sat down by the fire.

"I have made up my mind, sir," he began, bending forward as soon as we were seated, and speaking in a tone but a little above a whisper, "that you shall not have to ask me twice what troubles me. I took you for some one else yesterday evening. That troubles me."

"That mistake?"

"No. That some one else."

"Who is it?"

"I don't know."

"Like me?"

"I don't know. I never saw the face. The left arm is across the face, and the right arm is waved. Violently waved. This way."

I followed his action with my eyes, and it was the action of an arm gesticulating with the utmost passion and vehemence: "For God's sake clear the way!"

"One moonlight night," said the man, "I was sitting here, when I heard a voice cry, 'Halloa! Below there!' I started up, looked from that door, and saw this Some one else standing by the red light near the tunnel, waving as I just now showed you. The voice seemed hoarse with shouting, and it cried, 'Look out! Look out!' And then again, 'Halloa! Below there! Look out!' I caught up my lamp, turned it on red, and ran towards the figure, calling, 'What's wrong? What has happened? Where?' It stood just outside the blackness of the tunnel. I advanced so close upon it that I wondered at its keeping the sleeve across its eyes. I ran right up at it, and had my hand stretched out to pull the sleeve away, when it was gone."

"Into the tunnel?" said I.

"No. I ran on into the tunnel, five hundred yards. I stopped and held my lamp above my head, and saw the figures of the measured distance, and saw the wet stains stealing down the walls and trickling through the arch. I ran out again, faster than I had run in (for I had a mortal abhorrence of the place upon me), and I looked all round the red light with my own red light, and I went up the iron ladder to the gallery atop of it, and I came down again, and ran back here. I telegraphed both ways, 'An alarm has been given. Is anything wrong?' The answer came back, both ways, 'All well.'"

Resisting the slow touch of a frozen finger tracing out my spine, I showed him how that this figure must be a deception of his sense of sight, and how that figures, originating in disease of the delicate nerves that minister to the functions of the eye, were known to have often troubled patients, some of whom had become conscious of the nature of their affliction, and had even proved it by experiments upon themselves. "As to an imaginary cry," said I, "do but listen for a moment to the wind in this unnatural valley while we speak so low, and to the wild harp it makes of the telegraph wires!"

That was all very well, he returned, after we had sat listening for a while, and he ought to know something of the wind and the wires, he who so often passed long winter nights there, alone and watching. But he would beg to remark that he had not finished.

I asked his pardon, and he slowly added these words, touching my arm:—

"Within six hours after the Appearance, the memorable accident on this Line happened, and within ten hours the dead and wounded were brought along through the tunnel over the spot where the figure had stood."

A disagreeable shudder crept over me, but I did my best against it. It was not to be denied, I rejoined, that this was a remarkable coincidence, calculated deeply to impress the mind. But it was unquestionable that remarkable coincidences did continually occur, and they must be taken into account in dealing with such a subject. Though to be sure I must admit, I added (for I thought I saw that he was going to bring the objection to bear upon me), men of common-sense did not allow much for coincidences in making the ordinary calculations of life.

He again begged to remark that he had not finished.

I again begged his pardon for being betrayed into interruptions.

"This," he said, again laying his hand upon my arm, and glancing over his shoulder with hollow eyes, "was just a year ago. Six or seven months passed, and I had recovered from the surprise and shock, when one morning, as the day was breaking, I, standing at that door, looked towards the red light, and saw the spectre again." He stopped, with a fixed look at me.

"Did it cry out?"

"No. It was silent."

"Did it wave its arm?"

"No. It leaned against the shaft of the light, with both hands before the face. Like this."

79

Once more, I followed his action with my eyes. It was an action of mourning. I have seen such an attitude in stone figures on tombs.

"Did you go up to it?"

"I came in and sat down, partly to collect my thoughts, partly because it had turned me faint. When I went to the door again, daylight was above me, and the ghost was gone."

"But nothing followed? Nothing came of this?"

He touched me on the arm with his forefinger twice or thrice, giving a ghastly nod each time.

"That very day, as a train came out of the tunnel, I noticed, at a carriage window on my side, what looked like a confusion of hands and heads, and something waved. I saw it just in time to signal the driver, Stop! He shut off, and put his brake on, but the train drifted past here a hundred and fifty yards or more. I ran after it, and as I went along heard terrible screams and cries. A beautiful young lady had died instantaneously in one of the compartments, and was brought in here, and laid down on this floor between us."

Involuntarily I pushed my chair back, as I looked from the boards at which he pointed, to himself.

"True, sir. True. Precisely as it happened, so I tell it you."

I could think of nothing to say, to any purpose, and my mouth was very dry. The wind and the wires took up the story with a long lamenting wail.

He resumed. "Now, sir, mark this, and judge how my mind is troubled. The spectre came back, a week ago. Ever since, it has been there, now and again, by fits and starts."

"At the light?"

"At the Danger-light."

"What does it seem to do?"

He repeated, if possible with increased passion and vehemence, that former gesticulation of "For God's sake clear the way!"

Then he went on. "I have no peace or rest for it. It calls to me, for

80

many minutes together, in an agonized manner, 'Below there! Look out! Look out!' It stands waving to me. It rings my little bell—"

I caught at that. "Did it ring your bell yesterday evening when I was here, and you went to the door?"

"Twice."

"Why, see," said I, "how your imagination misleads you. My eyes were on the bell, and my ears were open to the bell, and, if I am a living man, it did NOT ring at those times. No, nor at any other time, except when it was rung in the natural course of physical things by the station communicating with you."

He shook his head. "I have never made a mistake as to that, yet, sir. I have never confused the spectre's ring with the man's. The ghost's ring is a strange vibration in the bell that it derives from nothing else, and I have not asserted that the bell stirs to the eye. I don't wonder that you failed to hear it. But I heard it."

"And did the spectre seem to be there, when you looked out?"

"It WAS there."

"Both times?"

He repeated firmly: "Both times."

"Will you come to the door with me, and look for it now?"

He bit his under-lip as though he were somewhat unwilling, but arose. I opened the door, and stood on the step, while he stood in the doorway. There was the Danger-light. There was the dismal mouth of the tunnel. There were the high wet stone walls of the cutting. There were the stars above them.

"Do you see it?" I asked him, taking particular note of his face. His eyes were prominent and strained; but not very much more so, perhaps, than my own had been when I had directed them earnestly towards the same point.

"No," he answered. "It is not there."

"Agreed," said I.

We went in again, shut the door, and resumed our seats. I was thinking how best to improve this advantage, if it might be called one, when he took up the conversation in such a matter-of-course way, so assuming that there could be no serious question of fact between us, that I felt myself placed in the weakest of positions.

"By this time you will fully understand, sir," he said, "that what troubles me so dreadfully is the question, What does the spectre mean?"

I was not sure, I told him, that I did fully understand.

"What is its warning against?" he said, ruminating, with his eyes on the fire, and only by times turning them on me. "What is the danger? Where is the danger? There is danger overhanging, somewhere on the Line. Some dreadful calamity will happen. It is not to be doubted this third time, after what has gone before. But surely this is a cruel haunting of me. What can I do?"

He pulled out his handkerchief, and wiped the drops from his heated forehead.

"If I telegraph Danger on either side of me, or on both, I can give no reason for it," he went on, wiping the palms of his hands. "I should get into trouble, and do no good. They would think I was mad. This is the way it would work:—Message: 'Danger! Take care!' Answer: 'What Danger? Where?' Message: 'Don't know. But for God's sake take care!' They would displace me. What else could they do?"

His pain of mind was most pitiable to see. It was the mental torture of a conscientious man, oppressed beyond endurance by an unintelligible responsibility involving life.

"When it first stood under the Danger-light," he went on, putting his dark hair back from his head, and drawing his hands outward across and across his temples in an extremity of feverish distress, "why not tell me where that accident was to happen,—if it must happen? Why not tell me how it could be averted,—if it could have been averted? When on its second coming it hid its face, why not tell me instead: 'She is going to die. Let them keep her at home'? If it came, on those two occasions, only to show me that its warnings were true, and so to prepare me for the third, why not warn me plainly now? And I, Lord help me! A mere poor signal-man on this solitary station! Why not go to somebody with credit to be believed, and power to act?"

82

When I saw him in this state, I saw that for the poor man's sake, as well as for the public safety, what I had to do for the time was to compose his mind. Therefore, setting aside all question of reality or unreality between us, I represented to him that whoever thoroughly discharged his duty must do well, and that at least it was his comfort that he understood his duty, though he did not understand these confounding Appearances. In this effort I succeeded far better than in the attempt to reason him out of his conviction. He became calm; the occupations incidental to his post, as the night advanced, began to make larger demands on his attention; and I left him at two in the morning. I had offered to stay through the night, but he would not hear of it.

That I more than once looked back at the red light as I ascended the pathway, that I did not like the red light, and that I should have slept but poorly if my bed had been under it, I see no reason to conceal. Nor did I like the two sequences of the accident and the dead girl. I see no reason to conceal that, either.

But what ran most in my thoughts was the consideration, how ought I to act, having become the recipient of this disclosure? I had proved the man to be intelligent, vigilant, painstaking, and exact; but how long might he remain so, in his state of mind? Though in a subordinate position, still he held a most important trust, and would I (for instance) like to stake my own life on the chances of his continuing to execute it with precision?

Unable to overcome a feeling that there would be something treacherous in my communicating what he had told me to his superiors in the Company, without first being plain with himself and proposing a middle course to him, I ultimately resolved to offer to accompany him (otherwise keeping his secret for the present) to the wisest medical practitioner we could hear of in those parts, and to take his opinion. A change in his time of duty would come round next night, he had apprised me, and he would be off an hour or two after sunrise, and on again soon after sunset. I had appointed to return accordingly.

Next evening was a lovely evening, and I walked out early to enjoy it. The sun was not yet quite down when I traversed the field-path near the top of the deep cutting. I would extend my walk for an hour, I said to myself, half an hour on and half an hour back, and it would then be time to go to my signal-man's box.

83

Before pursuing my stroll I stepped to the brink, and mechanically looked down, from the point from which I had first seen him. I cannot describe the thrill that seized upon me, when, close at the mouth of the tunnel, I saw the appearance of a man, with his left sleeve across his eyes, passionately waving his right arm.

The nameless horror that oppressed me passed in a moment, for in a moment I saw that this appearance of a man was a man indeed, and that there was a little group of other men standing at a short distance, to whom he seemed to be rehearsing the gesture he made. The Danger-light was not yet lighted. Against its shaft, a little low hut, entirely new to me, had been made of some wooden supports and tarpaulin. It looked no bigger than a bed.

With an irresistible sense that something was wrong, with a flashing self-reproachful fear that fatal mischief had come of my leaving the man there, and causing no one to be sent to overlook or correct what he did,—I descended the notched path with all the speed I could make.

"What is the matter?" I asked the men.

"Signal-man killed this morning, sir."

"Not the man belonging to that box?"

"Yes, sir."

"Not the man I know?"

"You will recognize him, sir, if you knew him," said the man who spoke for the others, solemnly uncovering his own head and raising an end of the tarpaulin, "for his face is quite composed."

"O, how did this happen, how did this happen?" I asked, turning from one to another as the hut closed in again.

"He was cut down by an engine, sir. No man in England knew his work better. But somehow he was not clear of the outer rail. It was just at broad day. He had struck the light, and had the lamp in his hand. As the engine came out of the tunnel, his back was towards her, and she cut him down. That man drove her, and was showing how it happened. Show the gentleman, Tom."

The man, who wore a rough, dark dress, stepped back to his former place at the mouth of the tunnel.

84

"Coming round the curve in the tunnel, sir," he said, "I saw him at the end, like as if I saw him down a perspective-glass. There was no time to check speed, and I knew him to be very careful. As he didn't seem to take heed of the whistle, I shut it off when we were running down upon him, and called to him as loud as I could call."

"What did you say?"

"I said, Below there! Look out! Look out! For God's sake, clear the way!"

I started.

"Ah! it was a dreadful time, sir. I never left off calling to him. I put this arm before my eyes, not to see, and I waved this arm to the last; but it was no use."

Without prolonging the narrative to dwell on any one of its curious circumstances more than on any other, I may, in closing it, point out the coincidence that the warning of the Engine-Driver included, not only the words which the unfortunate signal-man had repeated to me as haunting him, but also the words which I myself—not he—had attached, and that only in my own mind, to the gesticulation he had imitated.

THE HAUNTED SHIPS

BY ALLAN CUNNINGHAM

Along the sea of Solway, romantic on the Scottish side, with its woodlands, its bays, its cliffs, and headlands,—and interesting on the English side, with its many beautiful towns with their shadows on the water, rich pastures, safe harbors, and numerous ships,— there still linger many traditional stories of a maritime nature, most of them connected with superstitions singularly wild and unusual. To the curious these tales afford a rich fund of entertainment, from the many diversities of the same story; some dry and barren, and stripped of all the embellishments of poetry; others dressed out in all the riches of a superstitious belief and haunted imagination. In this they resemble the inland traditions of the peasants; but many of the oral treasures of the Galwegian or the Cumbrian coast have the stamp of the Dane and the Norseman upon them, and claim but a remote or faint affinity with the legitimate legends of Caledonia. Something like a rude prosaic outline of several of the most noted of the Northern ballads, the adventures and depredations of the old ocean kings, still lends life to the evening tale; and among others, the story of the Haunted Ships is still popular among the maritime peasantry.

One fine harvest evening I went on board the shallop of Richard Faulder, of Allanbay; and, committing ourselves to the waters, we allowed a gentle wind from the east to waft us at its pleasure toward the Scottish coast. We passed the sharp promontory of Siddick; and skirting the land within a stone-cast, glided along the shore till we came within sight of the ruined Abbey of Sweetheart. The green mountain of Criffell ascended beside us; and the bleat of the flocks from its summit, together with the winding of the evening horn of the reapers, came softened into something like music over land and sea. We pushed our shallop into a deep and wooded bay, and sat silently looking on the serene beauty of the place. The moon glimmered in her rising through the tall shafts of the pines of Caerlaverock; and the sky, with scarce a cloud, showered down on wood, and headland, and bay, the twinkling beams of a thousand stars, rendering every object visible. The tide, too, was coming with that swift and silent swell observable when the wind is gentle; the woody curves along the land were filling with the flood, till it touched the green branches of the drooping trees; while in the centre current the roll and the plunge of a thousand pellocks told to the experienced fisherman that salmon were abundant.

As we looked, we saw an old man emerging from a path that winded to the shore through a grove of doddered hazel; he carried a halvenet on his back, while behind him came a girl, bearing a small harpoon with which the fishers are remarkably dexterous in striking their prey. The senior seated himself on a large gray stone, which overlooked the bay, laid aside his bonnet, and submitted his bosom and neck to the refreshing sea-breeze; and taking his harpoon from his attendant, sat with the gravity and composure of a spirit of the flood, with his ministering nymph behind him. We pushed our shallop to the shore, and soon stood at their side.

"This is old Mark Macmoran, the mariner, with his grand-daughter Barbara," said Richard Faulder, in a whisper that had something of fear in it; "he knows every creek and cavern and quicksand in Solway,—has seen the Spectre Hound that haunts the Isle of Man; has heard him bark, and at every bark has seen a ship sink; and he has seen, too, the Haunted Ships in full sail; and, if all tales be true, he has sailed in them himself: he's an awful person."

Though I perceived in the communication of my friend something of the superstition of the sailor, I could not help thinking that common rumor had made a happy choice in singling out old Mark to maintain her intercourse with the invisible world. His hair, which seemed to have refused all intercourse with the comb, hung matted upon his shoulders; a kind of mantle, or rather blanket, pinned with a wooden skewer round his neck, fell mid-leg down, concealing all his nether garments as far as a pair of hose, darned with yarn of all conceivable colors, and a pair of shoes, patched and repaired till nothing of the original structure remained, and clasped on his feet with two massy silver buckles. If the dress of the old man was rude and sordid, that of his grand-daughter was gay, and even rich. She wore a bodice of fine wool, wrought round the bosom with alternate leaf and lily, and a kirtle of the same fabric, which, almost touching her white and delicate ankle, showed her snowy feet, so fairy-light and round that they scarcely seemed to touch the grass where she stood. Her hair, a natural ornament which woman seeks much to improve, was of bright glossy brown, and encumbered rather than

87

adorned with a snood, set thick with marine productions, among which the small clear pearl found in the Solway was conspicuous. Nature had not trusted to a handsome shape, and a sylph-like air, for young Barbara's influence over the heart of man; but had bestowed a pair of large bright blue eyes, swimming in liquid light, so full of love and gentleness and joy, that all the sailors from Annanwater to far Saint Bees acknowledged their power, and sung songs about the bonnie lass of Mark Macmoran. She stood holding a small gaff-hook of polished steel in her hand, and seemed not dissatisfied with the glances I bestowed on her from time to time, and which I held more than requited by a single glance of those eyes which retained so many capricious hearts in subjection.

The tide, though rapidly augmenting, had not yet filled the bay at our feet. The moon now streamed fairly over the tops of Caerlaverock pines, and showed the expanse of ocean dimpling and swelling, on which sloops and shallops came dancing, and displaying at every turn their extent of white sail against the beam of the moon. I looked on old Mark the Mariner, who, seated motionless on his gray stone, kept his eye fixed on the increasing waters with a look of seriousness and sorrow in which I saw little of the calculating spirit of a mere fisherman. Though he looked on the coming tide, his eyes seemed to dwell particularly on the black and decayed hulls of two vessels, which, half immersed in the quicksand, still addressed to every heart a tale of shipwreck and desolation. The tide wheeled and foamed around them; and creeping inch by inch up the side, at last fairly threw its waters over the top, and a long and hollow eddy showed the resistance which the liquid element received.

The moment they were fairly buried in the water, the old man clasped his hands together, and said, "Blessed be the tide that will break over and bury ye forever! Sad to mariners, and sorrowful to maids and mothers, has the time been you have choked up this deep and bonnie bay. For evil were you sent, and for evil have you continued. Every season finds from you its song of sorrow and wail, its funeral processions, and its shrouded corses. Woe to the land where the wood grew that made ye! Cursed be the axe that hewed ye on the mountains, the hands that joined ye together, the bay that ye first swam in, and the wind that wafted ye here! Seven times have ye put my life in peril, three fair sons have you swept from my side, and two bonnie grand-bairns; and now, even now, your waters foam and flash for my destruction, did I venture my infirm limbs in quest of food in your deadly bay. I see by that ripple and that foam, and hear by the sound and singing of your surge, that ye yearn for another victim; but it shall not be me nor mine."

Even as the old mariner addressed himself to the wrecked ships, a young man appeared at the southern extremity of the bay, holding his halve-net in his hand, and hastening into the current. Mark rose, and shouted, and waved him back from a place which, to a person unacquainted with the dangers of the bay, real and superstitious, seemed sufficiently perilous: his grand-daughter, too, added her voice to his, and waved her white hands; but the more they strove, the faster advanced the peasant, till he stood to his middle in the water, while the tide increased every moment in depth and strength. "Andrew, Andrew," cried the young woman, in a voice quavering with emotion, "turn, turn, I tell you: O the ships, the Haunted Ships!" But the appearance of a fine run of fish had more influence with the peasant than the voice of bonnie Barbara, and forward he dashed, net in hand. In a moment he was borne off his feet, and mingled like foam with the water, and hurried toward the fatal eddies which whirled and roared round the sunken ships. But he was a powerful young man, and an expert swimmer: he seized on one of the projecting ribs of the nearest hulk, and clinging to it with the grasp of despair, uttered yell after yell, sustaining himself against the prodigious rush of the current.

From a shealing of turf and straw, within the pitch of a bar from the spot where we stood, came out an old woman bent with age, and leaning on a crutch. "I heard the voice of that lad Andrew Lammie; can the chield be drowning, that he skirls sae uncannilie?" said the old woman, seating herself on the ground, and looking earnestly at the water. "Ou aye," she continued, "he's doomed, he's doomed; heart and hand can never save him; boats, ropes, and man's strength, and wit, all vain! vain! he's doomed, he's doomed!"

By this time I had thrown myself into the shallop, followed reluctantly by Richard Faulder, over whose courage and kindness of heart superstition had great power; and with one push from the shore, and some exertion in sculling, we came within a quoitcast of the unfortunate fisherman. He stayed not to profit by our aid; for when he perceived us near, he uttered a piercing shriek of joy, and bounded toward us through the agitated element the full length of an oar. I saw him for a second on the surface of the water; but the eddying current sucked him down; and all I ever beheld of him again was his hand held above the flood, and clutching in agony at some imaginary aid. I sat gazing in horror on the vacant sea before us: but a breathing time before, a human being, full of youth and strength and hope, was there: his cries were still ringing in my ears and echoing in the woods; and now nothing was seen or heard save the turbulent expanse of water, and the sound of its chafing on the shores. We pushed back our shallop, and resumed our station on the cliff beside the old mariner and his descendant.

"Wherefore sought ye to peril your own lives fruitlessly," said Mark, "in attempting to save the doomed? Whoso touches those infernal ships, never survives to tell the tale. Woe to the man who is found nigh them at midnight when the tide has subsided, and they arise in their former beauty, with forecastle, and deck, and sail, and pennon, and shroud! Then is seen the streaming of lights along the water from their cabin windows, and then is heard the sound of mirth and the clamor of tongues, and the infernal whoop and halloo, and song, ringing far and wide. Woe to the man who comes nigh them!"

To all this my Allanbay companion listened with a breathless attention. I felt something touched with a superstition to which I partly believed I had seen one victim offered up; and I inquired of the old mariner, "How and when came these haunted ships there? To me they seem but the melancholy relics of some unhappy voyagers, and much more likely to warn people to shun destruction, than entice and delude them to it."

"And so," said the old man with a smile, which had more of sorrow in it than of mirth,—"and so, young man, these black and shattered hulks seem to the eye of the multitude. But things are not what they seem: that water, a kind and convenient servant to the wants of man, which seems so smooth, and so dimpling, and so gentle, has swallowed up a human soul even now; and the place which it covers, so fair and so level, is a faithless quicksand, out of which none escape. Things are otherwise than they seem. Had you lived as long as I have had the sorrow to live; had you seen the storms, and braved the perils, and endured the distresses which have befallen me; had you sat gazing out on the dreary ocean at midnight on a haunted coast; had you seen comrade after comrade, brother after brother, and son after son, swept away by the merciless ocean from your very side; had you seen the shapes of friends, doomed to the wave and the quicksand, appearing to you in the dreams and visions of the night,—then would your mind have been prepared for

90

crediting the maritime legends of mariners; and the two haunted Danish ships would have had their terrors for you, as they have for all who sojourn on this coast.

"Of the time and the cause of their destruction," continued the old man, "I know nothing certain: they have stood as you have seen them for uncounted time; and while all other ships wrecked on this unhappy coast have gone to pieces, and rotted, and sunk away in a few years, these two haunted hulks have neither sunk in the quicksand, nor has a single spar or board been displaced. Maritime legend says, that two ships of Denmark having had permission, for a time, to work deeds of darkness and dolor on the deep, were at last condemned to the whirlpool and the sunken rock, and were wrecked in this bonnie bay, as a sign to seamen to be gentle and devout. The night when they were lost was a harvest evening of uncommon mildness and beauty: the sun had newly set; the moon came brighter and brighter out; and the reapers, laying their sickles at the root of the standing corn, stood on rock and bank, looking at the increasing magnitude of the waters, for sea and land were visible from Saint Bees to Barnhourie. The sails of two vessels were soon seen bent for the Scottish coast; and with a speed outrunning the swiftest ship, they approached the dangerous quicksands and headland of Borranpoint. On the deck of the foremost ship not a living soul was seen, or shape, unless something in darkness and form resembling a human shadow could be called a shape, which flitted from extremity to extremity of the ship, with the appearance of trimming the sails, and directing the vessel's course. But the decks of its companion were crowded with human shapes: the captain, and mate, and sailor, and cabin-boy, all seemed there; and from them the sound of mirth and minstrelsy echoed over land and water. The coast which they skirted along was one of extreme danger; and the reapers shouted to warn them to beware of sandbank and rock; but of this friendly counsel no notice was taken, except that a large and famished dog, which sat on the prow, answered every shout with a long, loud, and melancholy howl. The deep sandbank of Carsethorn was expected to arrest the career of these desperate navigators; but they passed, with the celerity of waterfowl, over an obstruction which had wrecked many pretty ships.

"Old men shook their heads and departed, saying, 'We have seen the fiend sailing in a bottomless ship; let us go home and pray': but one young and wilful man said, 'Fiend! I'll warrant it's nae fiend, but douce Janet Withershins, the witch, holding a carouse with some of her Cumberland cummers, and mickle red wine will be spilt atween them. Dod I would gladly have a toothfu'! I'll warrant it's nane o' your cauld, sour slae-water, like a bottle of Bailie Skrinkie's port, but right drap-o'-my-heart's-blood stuff, that would waken a body out of their last linen. I wonder where the cummers will anchor their craft?'—'And I'll vow,' said another rustic, 'the wine they quaff is none of your visionary drink, such as a drouthie body has dished out to his lips in a dream; nor is it shadowy and unsubstantial, like the vessels they sail in, which are made out of a cockleshell or a cast-off slipper, or the paring of a seaman's right thumb-nail. I once got a hansel out of a witch's quaigh myself,—auld Marion Mathers, of Dustiefoot, whom they tried to bury in the old kirkyard of Dunscore, but the cummer raise as fast as they laid her down, and naewhere else would she lie but in the bonnie green kirkyard of Kier, among douce and sponsible fowk. So I'll vow that the wine of a witch's cup is as fell liquor as ever did a kindly turn to a poor man's heart; and be they fiends, or be they witches, if they have red wine asteer, I'll risk a drouket sark for ae glorious tout on't.'—'Silence, ye sinners,' said the minister's son of a neighboring parish, who united in his own person his father's lack of devotion with his mother's love of liquor. 'Whisht!—speak as if ye had the fear of something holy before ye. Let the vessels run their own way to destruction: who can stay the eastern wind, and the current of the Solway sea? I can find ye Scripture warrant for that: so let them try their strength on Blawhooly rocks, and their might on the broad quicksand. There's a surf running there would knock the ribs together of a galley built by the imps of the pit, and commanded by the Prince of Darkness. Bonnilie and bravely they sail away there; but before the blast blows by they'll be wrecked: and red wine and strong brandy will be as rife as dyke-water, and we'll drink the health of bonnie Bell Blackness out of her left-foot slipper.'

"The speech of the young profligate was applauded by several of his companions, and away they flew to the bay of Blawhooly, from whence they never returned. The two vessels were observed all at once to stop in the bosom of the bay on the spot where their hulls now appear: the mirth and the minstrelsy waxed louder than ever; and the forms of maidens, with instruments of music, and wine-cups in their hands, thronged the decks. A boat was lowered; and the same shadowy pilot who conducted the ships made it start toward the shore with the rapidity of lightning, and its head knocked against the bank where the four young men stood, who longed for the unblest drink. They leaped in with a laugh, and with a laugh were they welcomed on deck; wine-cups were given to each, and as they raised them to their lips the vessels melted away beneath their feet; and one loud shriek, mingled with laughter still louder, was heard over land and water for many miles. Nothing more was heard or seen till the morning, when the crowd who came to the beach saw with fear and wonder the two Haunted Ships, such as they now seem, masts and tackle gone; nor mark, nor sign, by which their name, country, or destination could be known, was left remaining. Such is the tradition of the mariners; and its truth has been attested by many families whose sons and whose fathers have been drowned in the haunted bay of Blawhooly."

"And trow ye," said the old woman, who, attracted from her hut by the drowning cries of the young fisherman, had remained an auditor of the mariner's legend,—"and trow ye, Mark Macmoran, that the tale of the Haunted Ships is done? I can say no to that. Mickle have mine ears heard; but more mine eyes have witnessed since I came to dwell in this humble home by the side of the deep sea. I mind the night weel: it was on Hallowmass eve: the nuts were cracked, and the apples were eaten, and spell and charm were tried at my fireside; till, wearied with diving into the dark waves of futurity, the lads and lasses fairly took to the more visible blessings of kind words, tender clasps, and gentle courtship. Soft words in a maiden's ear, and a kindly kiss o' her lip, were old-world matters to me, Mark Macmoran; though I mean not to say that I have been free of the folly of daunering and daffin with a youth in my day, and keeping tryste with him in dark and lonely places. However, as I say, these times of enjoyment were passed and gone with me; the mair's the pity that pleasure should fly sae fast away,—and as I could nae make sport I thought I should not mar any; so out I sauntered into the fresh cold air, and sat down behind that old oak, and looked abroad on the wide sea. I had my ain sad thoughts, ye may think, at the time: it was in that very bay my blythe goodman perished, with seven more in his company, and on that very bank where ye see the waves leaping and foaming, I saw seven stately corses streeked, but the dearest was the eighth. It was a woful sight to me, a widow, with four bonnie boys, with nought to support them but these twa hands, and God's blessing, and a cow's grass. I have never liked to live out of sight of this bay since that time; and mony's the moonlight night I sit looking on these watery mountains, and these waste shores; it does my heart good, whatever it may do to my head. So ye see it was Hallowmass night; and looking on sea and land sat I; and my heart wandering to other thoughts soon made me forget my youthful company at hame. It might be near the howe hour of the night; the tide was making, and its singing brought strange old-world stories with it; and I thought on the dangers that sailors endure, the fates they meet with, and the fearful forms they see. My own blythe goodman had seen sights that made him grave enough at times, though he aye tried to laugh them away.

"Aweel, atween that very rock aneath us and the coming tide, I saw, or thought I saw, for the tale is so dream-like, that the whole might pass for a vision of the night, I saw the form of a man: his plaid was gray; his face was gray; and his hair, which hung low down till it nearly came to the middle of his back, was as white as the white sea-foam. He began to howk and dig under the bank; an' God be near me, thought I, this maun be the unblessed spirit of Auld Adam Gowdgowpin, the miser, who is doomed to dig for shipwrecked treasure, and count how many millions are hidden forever from man's enjoyment. The Form found something which in shape and hue seemed a left-foot slipper of brass; so down to the tide he marched, and placing it on the water, whirled it thrice round; and the infernal slipper dilated at every turn, till it became a bonnie barge with its sails bent, and on board leaped the form, and scudded swiftly away. He came to one of the Haunted Ships; and striking it with his oar, a fair ship, with mast, and canvas, and mariners, started up: he touched the other Haunted Ship, and produced the like transformation; and away the three spectre ships bounded, leaving a track of fire behind them on the billows which was long unextinguished. Now was nae that a bonnie and a fearful sight to see beneath the light of the Hallowmass moon? But the tale is far frae finished; for mariners say that once a year, on a certain night, if ye stand on the Borranpoint, ye will see the infernal shallops coming snoring through the Solway; ye will hear the same laugh, and song, and mirth, and minstrelsy, which our ancestors heard; see them bound over the sandbanks and sunken rocks like sea-gulls, cast their anchor in Blawhooly Bay, while the shadowy figure lowers down the boat, and augments their numbers with the four unhappy mortals, to whose memory a stone stands in the kirkyard, with a sinking ship and a shoreless sea cut upon it. Then the spectre ships vanish, and the drowning shriek of mortals and the rejoicing laugh of fiends are heard, and the old hulls are left as a memorial that the old spiritual kingdom has not departed from the earth. But I maun away, and trim my little cottage fire, and make it burn and blaze up bonnie, to warm the crickets, and my cold and crazy bones, that maun soon be laid aneath the green sod in the eerie kirkyard." And away the old dame tottered to her cottage, secured the door on the inside, and soon the hearth-flame was seen to glimmer and gleam through the key-hole and window.

"I'll tell ye what," said the old mariner, in a subdued tone, and with a shrewd and suspicious glance of his eye after the old sibyl, "it's a word that may not very well be uttered, but there are many mistakes made in evening stories if old Moll Moray there, where she lives, knows not mickle more than she is willing to tell of the Haunted Ships and their unhallowed mariners. She lives cannilie and quietly; no one knows how she is fed or supported; but her dress is aye whole, her cottage ever smokes, and her table lacks neither of wine, white and red, nor of fowl and fish, and white bread and brown. It was a dear scoff to Jock Matheson, when he called old Moll the uncannie carline of Blawhooly: his boat ran round and round in the centre of the Solway,—everybody said it was enchanted,—and down it went head foremost: and had nae Jock been a swimmer equal to a sheldrake, he would have fed the fish; but I'll warrant it sobered the lad's speech; and he never reckoned himself safe till he made auld Moll the present of a new kirtle and a stone of cheese."

"O father," said his grand-daughter Barbara, "ye surely wrong poor old Mary Moray; what use could it be to an old woman like her, who has no wrongs to redress, no malice to work out against mankind, and nothing to seek of enjoyment save a cannie hour and a quiet grave,—what use could the fellowship of fiends, and the communion of evil spirits, be to her? I know Jenny Primrose puts rowan-tree above the door-head when she sees old Mary coming; I know the good wife of Kittlenaket wears rowan-berry leaves in the headband of her blue kirtle, and all for the sake of averting the unsonsie glance of Mary's right ee; and I know that the auld laird of Burntroutwater drives his seven cows to their pasture with a wand of witch-tree, to keep Mary from milking them. But what has all that to do with haunted shallops, visionary mariners, and bottomless boats? I have heard myself as pleasant a tale about the Haunted Ships and their unworldly crews, as any one would wish to hear in a winter evening. It was told me by young Benjie Macharg, one summer night, sitting on Arbiglandbank: the lad intended a sort of love meeting; but all that he could talk of was about smearing sheep and shearing sheep, and of the wife which the Norway elves of the Haunted Ships made for his uncle Sandie Macharg. And I shall tell ye the tale as the honest lad told it to me.

95

"Alexander Macharg, besides being the laird of three acres of peatmoss, two kale gardens, and the owner of seven good milch cows, a pair of horses, and six pet sheep, was the husband of one of the handsomest women in seven parishes. Many a lad sighed the day he was brided; and a Nithsdale laird and two Annandale moorland farmers drank themselves to their last linen, as well as their last shilling, through sorrow for her loss. But married was the dame; and home she was carried, to bear rule over her home and her husband, as an honest woman should. Now ye maun ken that though the flesh and blood lovers of Alexander's bonnie wife all ceased to love and to sue her after she became another's, there were certain admirers who did not consider their claim at all abated, or their hopes lessened, by the kirk's famous obstacle of matrimony. Ye have heard how the devout minister of Tinwald had a fair son carried away, and bedded against his liking to an unchristened bride, whom the elves and the fairies provided; ye have heard how the bonnie bride of the drunken laird of Soukitup was stolen by the fairies out at the back-window of the bridal chamber, the time the bridegroom was groping his way to the chamber-door; and ye have heard— But why need I multiply cases? such things in the ancient days were as common as candle-light. So ye'll no hinder certain water-elves and sea-fairies, who sometimes keep festival and summer mirth in these old haunted hulks, from falling in love with the weel-faured wife of Laird Macharg; and to their plots and contrivances they went how they might accomplish to sunder man and wife; and sundering such a man and such a wife was like sundering the green leaf from the summer, or the fragrance from the flower.

"So it fell on a time that Laird Macharg took his halve-net on his back, and his steel spear in his hand, and down to Blawhooly Bay gaed he, and into the water he went right between the two haunted hulks, and placing his net awaited the coming of the tide. The night, ye maun ken, was mirk, and the wind lowne, and the singing of the increasing waters among the shells and the pebbles was heard for sundry miles. All at once lights began to glance and twinkle on board the two Haunted Ships from every hole and seam, and presently the sound as of a hatchet employed in squaring timber echoed far and wide. But if the toil of these unearthly workmen amazed the Laird, how much more was his amazement increased when a sharp shrill voice called out, 'Ho! brother, what are you doing now?' A voice still shriller responded from the other haunted ship, 'I'm making a wife to Sandie Macharg!' and a loud quavering laugh running from ship to ship, and from bank to bank, told the joy they expected from their labor.

"Now the Laird, besides being a devout and a God-fearing man, was shrewd and bold; and in plot, and contrivance, and skill in conducting his designs, was fairly an overmatch for any dozen land-elves; but the water-elves are far more subtle; besides, their haunts and their dwellings being in the great deep, pursuit and detection is hopeless if they succeed in carrying their prey to the waves. But ye shall hear. Home flew the Laird, collected his family around the hearth, spoke of the signs and the sins of the times, and talked of mortification and prayer for averting calamity; and finally, taking his father's Bible, brass clasps, black print, and covered with calf-skin, from the shelf, he proceeded without let or stint to perform domestic worship. I should have told ye that he bolted and locked the door, shut up all inlet to the house, threw salt into the fire, and proceeded in every way like a man skilful in guarding against the plots of fairies and fiends. His wife looked on all this with wonder; but she saw something in her husband's looks that hindered her from intruding either question or advice, and a wise woman was she.

"Near the mid-hour of the night the rush of a horse's feet was heard, and the sound of a rider leaping from its back, and a heavy knock came to the door, accompanied by a voice saying, 'The cummer drink's hot, and the knave bairn is expected at Laird Laurie's to-night; sae mount, goodwife, and come.'

"'Preserve me!' said the wife of Sandie Macharg; 'that's news indeed! who could have thought it? the Laird has been heirless for seventeen years! Now, Sandie, my man, fetch me my skirt and hood.'

"But he laid his arm round his wife's neck, and said, 'If all the lairds in Galloway go heirless, over this door threshold shall you not stir to-night; and I have said, and I have sworn it: seek not to know why or wherefore; but, Lord, send us thy blessed mornlight.' The wife looked for a moment in her husband's eyes, and desisted from further entreaty.

"'But let us send a civil message to the gossips, Sandie; and hadnae ye better say I am sair laid with a sudden sickness? though it's sinful-like to send the poor messenger a mile agate with a lie in his mouth without a glass of brandy.'

"'To such a messenger, and to those who sent him, no apology is needed,' said the austere Laird, 'so let him depart.' And the clatter of a horse's hoofs was heard, and the muttered imprecations of its rider on the churlish treatment he had experienced.

"'Now, Sandie, my lad,' said his wife, laying an arm particularly white and round about his neck as she spoke, 'are you not a queer man and a stern? I have been your wedded wife now these three years; and, beside my dower, have brought you three as bonnie bairns as ever smiled aneath a summer sun. O man, you a douce man, and fitter to be an elder than even Willie Greer himself, I have the minister's ain word for't, to put on these hard-hearted looks, and gang waving your arms that way, as if ye said, "I winna take the counsel of sic a hempie as you"; I'm your ain leal wife, and will and maun have an explanation.'

"To all this Sandie Macharg replied, 'It is written, "Wives, obey your husbands"; but we have been stayed in our devotion, so let us pray.' And down he knelt: his wife knelt also, for she was as devout as bonnie; and beside them knelt their household, and all lights were extinguished.

"'Now this beats a',' muttered his wife to herself; 'however, I shall be obedient for a time; but if I dinna ken what all this is for before the morn by sunset-time, my tongue is nae langer a tongue, nor my hands worth wearing.'

"The voice of her husband in prayer interrupted this mental soliloquy; and ardently did he beseech to be preserved from the wiles of the fiends, and the snares of Satan; 'from witches, ghosts, goblins, elves, fairies, spunkies, and water-kelpies; from the spectre shallop of Solway; from spirits visible and invisible; from the Haunted Ships and their unearthly tenants; from maritime spirits that plotted against godly men, and fell in love with their wives—'

"'Nay, but His presence be near us!' said his wife in a low tone of dismay. 'God guide my gudeman's wits: I never heard such a prayer from human lips before. But, Sandie, my man, Lord's sake, rise: what fearful light is this?—barn and byre and stable maun be in a blaze; and Hawkie and Hurley,—Doddie, and Cherrie, and Damson-plum, will be smoored with reek and scorched with flame.'

"And a flood of light, but not so gross as a common fire, which ascended to heaven and filled all the court before the house, amply justified the good wife's suspicions. But to the terrors of fire, Sandie was as immovable as he was to the imaginary groans of the barren wife of Laird Laurie; and he held his wife, and threatened the weight of his right hand—and it was a heavy one—to all who ventured abroad, or even unbolted the door. The neighing and prancing of horses, and the bellowing of cows, augmented the horrors of the night; and to any one who only heard the din, it seemed that the whole onstead was in a blaze, and horses and cattle perishing in the flame. All wiles, common or extraordinary, were put in practice to entice or force the honest farmer and his wife to open the door; and when the like success attended every new stratagem, silence for a little while ensued, and a long, loud, and shrilling laugh wound up the dramatic efforts of the night. In the morning, when Laird Macharg went to the door, he found standing against one of the pilasters a piece of black ship oak, rudely fashioned into something like human form, and which skilful people declared would have been clothed with seeming flesh and blood, and palmed upon him by elfin adroitness for his wife, had he admitted his visitants. A synod of wise men and women sat upon the woman of timber, and she was finally ordered to be devoured by fire, and that in the open air. A fire was soon made, and into it the elfin sculpture was tossed from the prongs of two pairs of pitchforks. The blaze that arose was awful to behold; and hissings, and burstings, and loud cracklings, and strange noises, were heard in the midst of the flame; and when the whole sank into ashes, a drinking-cup of some precious metal was found; and this cup, fashioned no doubt by elfin skill, but rendered harmless by the purification with fire, the sons and daughters of Sandie Macharg and his wife drink out of to this very day. Bless all bold men, say I, and obedient wives!"

A RAFT THAT NO MAN MADE

BY ROBERT T. S. LOWELL

I am a soldier: but my tale, this time, is not of war.

The man of whom the Muse talked to the blind bard of old had grown wise in wayfaring. He had seen such men and cities as the sun shines on, and the great wonders of land and sea; and he had visited the farther countries, whose indwellers, having been once at home in the green fields and under the sky and roofs of the cheery earth, were now gone forth and forward into a dim and shadowed land, from which they found no backward path to these old haunts, and their old loves:

> 'Ήέρι καὶ νεφέλῃ κεκαλυμμένοι · οὐδέ ποτ' αὐτοὺς
> 'Ήέλιος φαέθων καταδέρκεται ἀκτίνεσσιν.

Od. XI.

At the Charter-House I learned the story of the King of Ithaca, and read it for something better than a task; and since, though I have never seen so many cities as the much-wandering man, nor grown so wise, yet have heard and seen and remembered, for myself, words and things from crowded streets and fairs and shows and wave-washed quays and murmurous market-places, in many lands; and for his Quote,—his people wrapt in cloud and vapor, whom "no glad sun finds with his beams,"—have been borne along a perilous path through thick mists, among the crashing ice of the Upper Atlantic, as well as sweltered upon a Southern sea, and have learned something of men and something of God.

I was in Newfoundland, a lieutenant of Royal Engineers, in Major Gore's time, and went about a good deal among the people, in surveying for Government. One of my old friends there was Skipper Benjie Westham, of Brigus, a shortish, stout, bald man, with a cheerful, honest face and a kind voice; and he, mending a caplin-seine one day, told me this story, which I will try to tell after him.

We were upon the high ground, beyond where the church stands

100

now, and Prudence, the fisherman's daughter, and Ralph Barrows, her husband, were with Skipper Benjie when he began; and I had an hour by the watch to spend. The neighborhood, all about, was still; the only men who were in sight were so far off that we heard nothing from them; no wind was stirring near us, and a slow sail could be seen outside. Everything was right for listening and telling.

"I can tell 'ee what I sid[1] myself, Sir," said Skipper Benjie. "It is n' like a story that's put down in books: it's on'y like what we planters[2] tells of a winter's night or sech: but it's feelun, mubbe, an' 'ee won't expect much off a man as could n' never read,—not so much as Bible or Prayer-Book, even."

Skipper Benjie looked just like what he was thought: a true-hearted, healthy man, a good fisherman and a good seaman. There was no need of any one's saying it. So I only waited till he went on speaking.

"'T was one time I goed to th' Ice, Sir. I never goed but once, an' 't was a'most the first v'yage ever was, ef 't was n' the very first; an' 't was the last for me, an' worse agen for the rest-part o' that crew, that never goed no more! 'T was tarrible sad douns wi' they!"

This preface was accompanied by some preliminary handling of the caplin-seine, also, to find out the broken places and get them about him. Ralph and Prudence deftly helped him. Then, making his story wait, after this opening, he took one hole to begin at in mending, chose his seat, and drew the seine up to his knee. At the same time I got nearer to the fellowship of the family by persuading the planter (who yielded with a pleasant smile) to let me try my hand at the netting. Prudence quietly took to herself a share of the work, and Ralph alone was unbusied.

"They calls th' Ice a wicked place,—Sundays an' weekin days all alike; an' to my seemun it's a cruel, bloody place, jes' so well,—but not all thinks alike, surely.—Rafe, lad, mubbe 'ee 'd ruther go down coveways, an' overhaul the punt a bit."

Ralph, who perhaps had stood waiting for the very dismissal that he now got, assented and left us three. Prudence, to be sure, looked after him as if she would a good deal rather go with him than stay; but she stayed, nevertheless, and worked at the seine. I interpreted

---

[1] Saw.
[2] Fishermen.

to myself Skipper Benjie's sending away of one of his hearers by supposing that his son-in-law had often heard his tales; but the planter explained himself:—

"'Ee sees, Sir, I knocked off goun to th' Ice becase 't was sech a tarrible cruel place, to my seemun. They swiles[3] be so knowun like,—as knowun as a dog, in a manner, an' lovun to their own, like Christens, a'most, more than bastes; an' they'm got red blood, for all they lives most-partly in water; an' then I found 'em so friendly, when I was wantun friends badly. But I s'pose the swile-fishery's needful; an' I knows, in course, that even Christens' blood's got to be taken sometimes, when it's bad blood, an' I would n' be childish about they things: on'y—ef it's me—when I can live by fishun, I don' want to go an' club an' shoot an' cut an' slash among poor harmless things that 'ould never harm man or 'oman, an' 'ould cry great tears down for pity-sake, an' got a sound like a Christen: I 'ould n' like to go a-swilun for gain,—not after beun among 'em, way I was, anyways."

This apology made it plain that Skipper Benjie was large-hearted enough, or indulgent enough, not to seek to strain others, even his own family, up to his own way in everything; and it might easily be thought that the young fisherman had different feelings about sealing from those that the planter's story was meant to bring out. All being ready, he began his tale again:—

"I shipped wi' Skipper Isra'l Gooden, from Carbonear; the schooner was the Baccaloue, wi' forty men, all told. 'T was of a Sunday morn'n 'e 'ould sail, twel'th day o' March, wi' another schooner in company,—the Sparrow. There was a many of us was n' too good, but we thowt wrong of 'e's takun the Lord's Day to 'e'sself. Wull, Sir, afore I comed 'ome, I was in a great desert country, an' floated on sea wi' a monstrous great raft that no man never made, creakun an' crashun an' groanun an' tumblun an' wastun an' goun to pieces, an' no man on her but me, an' full o' livun things,—dreadful!

"About a five hours out, 't was, we first sid the blink,[4] an' comed up wi' th' Ice about off Cape Bonavis'. We fell in wi' it south, an' worked up nothe along: but we did n' see swiles for two or three days yet; on'y we was workun along; pokun the cakes of ice away, an' haulun through wi' main strength sometimes, holdun on wi' bights o' ropes

---

[3] Seals.
[4] A dull glare on the horizon, from the immense masses of ice.

out o' the bow; an' more times, agen, in clear water: sometimes mist all round us, 'ee could n' see the ship's len'th, sca'ce; an' more times snow, jes' so thick; an' then a gale o' wind, mubbe, would a'most blow all the spars out of her, seemunly.

"We kep' sight o' th' other schooner, most-partly; an' when we did n' keep it, we'd get it agen. So one night 't was a beautiful moonlight night: I think I never sid a moon so bright as that moon was; an' such lovely sights a body 'ould n' think could be! Little islands, an' bigger, agen, there was, on every hand, shinun so bright, wi' great, awful-lookun shadows! an' then the sea all black, between! They did look so beautiful as ef a body could go an' bide on 'em, in' a manner; an' the sky was jes' so blue, an' the stars all shinun out, an' the moon all so bright! I never looked upon the like. An' so I stood in the bows; an' I don' know ef I thowt o' God first, but I was thinkun o' my girl that I was troth-plight wi' then, an' a many things, when all of a sudden we comed upon the hardest ice we'd a-had; an' into it; an' then, wi' pokun an' haulun, workun along. An' there was a cry goed up,—like the cry of a babby, 't was, an' I thowt mubbe 't was a somethun had got upon one o' they islands; but I said, agen, 'How could it?' an' one John Harris said 'e thowt 't was a bird. Then another man (Moffis 'e's name was) started off wi' what they calls a gaff ('t is somethun like a short boat-hook), over the bows, an' run; an' we sid un strike, an' strike, an' we hard it go wump! wump! an' the cry goun up so tarrible feelun, seemed as ef 'e was murderun some poor wild Inden child 'e 'd a-found (on'y mubbe 'e would n' do so bad as that: but there 've a-been tarrible bloody, cruel work wi' Indens in my time), an' then 'e comed back wi' a white-coat[5] over 'e's shoulder; an' the poor thing was n' dead, but cried an' soughed like any poor little babby."

The young wife was very restless at this point, and, though she did not look up, I saw her tears. The stout fisherman smoothed out the net a little upon his knee, and drew it in closer, and heaved a great sigh: he did not look at his hearers.

"When 'e throwed it down, it walloped, an' cried, an' soughed,—an' its poor eyes blinded wi' blood! ('Ee sees, Sir," said the planter, by way of excusing his tenderness, "they swiles were friends to I, after.) Dear, O dear! I could n' stand it; for 'e might ha' killed un; an' so 'e goes for a quart o' rum, for fetchun first swile, an' I went an' put the

---

[5] A young seal.

poor thing out o' pain. I did n' want to look at they beautiful islands no more, somehow. Bumby it comed on thick, an' then snow.

"Nex' day swiles bawlun[6] every way, poor things! (I knowed their voice, now,) but 't was blowun a gale o' wind, an' we under bare poles, an' snow comun agen, so fast as ever it could come: but out the men 'ould go, all mad like, an' my watch goed, an' so I mus' go. (I did n' think what I was goun to!) The skipper never said no; but to keep near the schooner, an' fetch in first we could, close by; an' keep near the schooner.

"So we got abroad, an' the men that was wi' me jes' began to knock right an' left: 't was heartless to see an' hear it. They laved two old uns an' a young whelp to me, as they runned by. The mother did cry like a Christen, in a manner, an' the big tears 'ould run down, an' they 'ould both be so brave for the poor whelp that 'ould cuddle up an' cry; an' the mother looked this way an' that way, wi' big, pooty, black eyes, to see what was the manun of it, when they'd never doned any harm in God's world that 'E made, an' would n', even ef you killed 'em: on'y the poor mother baste ketched my gaff, that I was goun to strike wi', betwixt her teeth, an' I could n' get it away. 'T was n' like fishun! (I was weak-hearted like: I s'pose 't was wi' what was comun that I did n' know.) Then comed a hail, all of a sudden, from the schooner (we had n' been gone more 'n a five minutes, ef 't was so much,—no, not more 'n a three); but I was glad to hear it come then, however: an' so every man ran, one afore t' other. There the schooner was, tearun through all, an' we runnun for dear life. I falled among the slob,[7] and got out agen. 'T was another man pushun agen me doned it. I could n' 'elp myself from goun in, an' when I got out I was astarn of all, an' there was the schooner carryun on, right through to clear water! So, hold of a bight o' line, or anything! an' they swung up in over bows an' sides! an' swash! she struck the water, an' was out o' sight in a minute, an' the snow drivun as ef 't would bury her, an' a man laved behind on a pan of ice, an' the great black say two fathom ahead, an' the storm-wind blowun 'im into it!"

The planter stopped speaking. We had all gone along so with the story, that the stout seafarer, as he wrought the whole scene up about us, seemed instinctively to lean back and brace his feet

---

[6] Technical word for the crying of the seals.
[7] Broken ice, between large cakes, or against the shore.

against the ground, and clutch his net. The young woman looked up, this time; and the cold snow-blast seemed to howl through that still summer's noon, and the terrific ice-fields and hills to be crashing against the solid earth that we sat upon, and all things round changed to the far-off stormy ocean and boundless frozen wastes.

The planter began to speak again:—

"So I falled right down upon th' ice, sayun, 'Lard, help me! Lard, help me!' an' crawlun away, wi' the snow in my face (I was afeard, a'most, to stand), 'Lard, help me! Lard, help me!'

"'T was n' all hard ice, but many places lolly;[8] an' once I goed right down wi' my hand-wristès an' my armès in cold water, part-ways to the bottom o' th' ocean; and a'most head-first into un, as I'd a-been in wi' my legs afore: but, thanks be to God! 'E helped me out of un, but colder an' wetter agen.

"In course I wanted to folly the schooner; so I runned up along, a little ways from the edge, an' then I runned down along: but 't was all great black ocean outside, an' she gone miles an' miles away; an' by two hours' time, even ef she'd come to, itself, an' all clear weather, I could n' never see her; an' ef she could come back, she could n' never find me, more 'n I could find any one o' they flakes o' snow. The schooner was gone, an' I was laved out o' the world!

"Bumby, when I got on the big field agen, I stood up on my feet, an' I sid that was my ship! She had n' e'er a sail, an' she had n' e'er a spar, an' she had n' e'er a compass, an' she had n' e'er a helm, an' she had n' no hold, an' she had n' no cabin. I could n' sail her, nor I could n' steer her, nor I could n' anchor her, nor bring her to, but she would go, wind or calm, an' she'd never come to port, but out in th' ocean she'd go to pieces! I sid 't was so, an' I must take it, an' do my best wi' it. 'T was jest a great, white, frozen raft, driftun bodily away, wi' storm blowun over, an' current runnun under, an' snow comun down so thick, an' a poor Christen laved all alone wi' it. 'T would drift as long as anything was of it, an' 't was n' likely there'd be any life in the poor man by time th' ice goed to nawthun; an' the swiles 'ould swim back agen up to the Nothe!

"I was th' only one, seemunly, to be cast out alive, an' wi' the dearest maid in the world (so I thought) waitun for me. I s'pose 'ee might

---

[8] Snow in water, not yet frozen, but looking like the white ice.

ha' knowed somethun better, Sir; but I was n' larned, an' I ran so fast as ever I could up the way I thowt home was, an' I groaned, an' groaned, an' shook my handès, an' then I thowt, 'Mubbe I may be goun wrong way.' So I groaned to the Lard to stop the snow. Then I on'y ran this way an' that way, an' groaned for snow to knock off.[9] I knowed we was driftun mubbe a twenty leagues a day, and anyways I wanted to be doun what I could, keepun up over th' Ice so well as I could, Noofundland-ways, an' I might come to somethun,—to a schooner or somethun; anyways I'd get up so near as I could. So I looked for a lee. I s'pose 'ee 'd ha' knowed better what to do, Sir," said the planter, here again appealing to me, and showing by his question that he understood me, in spite of my pea-jacket.

I had been so carried along with his story that I had felt as if I were the man on the Ice, myself, and assured him, that, though I could get along pretty well on land, and could even do something at netting, I should have been very awkward in his place.

"Wull, Sir, I looked for a lee. ('T would n' ha' been so cold, to say cold, ef it had n' a-blowed so tarrible hard.) First step, I stumbled upon somethun in the snow, seemed soft, like a body! Then I comed all together, hopun an' fearun an' all together. Down I goed upon my knees to un, an' I smoothed away the snow, all tremblun, an' there was a moan, as ef 't was a-livun.

"'O Lard!' I said, 'who's this? Be this one of our men?'

"But how could it? So I scraped the snow away, but 't was easy to see 't was smaller than a man. There was n' no man on that dreadful place but me! Wull, Sir, 't was a poor swile, wi' blood runnun all under; an' I got my cuffs[10] an' sleeves all red wi' it. It looked like a fellow-creatur's blood, a'most, an' I was a lost man, left to die away out there in th' Ice, an' I said, 'Poor thing! poor thing!' an' I did n' mind about the wind, or th' ice, or the schooner goun away from me afore a gale (I would n' mind about 'em), an' a poor lost Christen may show a good turn to a hurt thing, ef 't was on'y a baste. So I smoothed away the snow wi' my cuffs, an' I sid 't was a poor thing wi' her whelp close by her, an' her tongue out, as ef she'd a-died fondlun an' lickun it; an' a great puddle o' blood,—it looked tarrible heartless, when I was so nigh to death, an' was n' hungry. An' then I feeled a stick, an' I thowt, 'It may be a help to me,' an' so I pulled un,

---

[9] To stop.
[10] Mittens.

106

an' it would n' come, an' I found she was lyun on it; so I hauled agen, an' when it comed, 't was my gaff the poor baste had got away from me, an' got it under her, an' she was a-lyun on it. Some o' the men, when they was runnun for dear life, must ha' struck 'em, out o' madness like, an' laved 'em to die where they was. 'T was the whelp was n' quite dead. 'Ee'll think 't was foolish, Sir, but it seemed as though they was somethun to me, an' I'd a-lost the last friendly thing there was.

"I found a big hummock an' sheltered under it, standun on my feet, wi' nawthun to do but think, an' think, an' pray to God; an' so I doned. I could n' help feelun to God then, surely. Nawthun to do, an' no place to go, tull snow cleared away; but jes' drift wi' the great Ice down from the Nothe, away down over the say, a sixty mile a day, mubbe. I was n' a good Christen, an' I could n' help a-thinkun o' home an' she I was troth-plight wi', an' I doubled over myself an' groaned,—I could n' help it; but bumby it comed into me to say my prayers, an' it seemed as thof she was askun me to pray (an' she was good, Sir, al'ays), an' I seemed all opened, somehow, an' I knowed how to pray."

While the words were coming tenderly from the weather-beaten fisherman, I could not help being moved, and glanced over toward the daughter's seat; but she was gone, and, turning round, I saw her going quietly, almost stealthily, and very quickly, toward the cove.

The father gave no heed to her leaving, but went on with his tale:—

"Then the wind began to fall down, an' the snow knocked off altogether, an' the sun comed out; an' I sid th' Ice, field-ice an' icebargs, an' every one of 'em flashun up as ef they'd kendled up a bonfire, but no sign of a schooner! no sign of a schooner! nor no sign o' man's douns, but on'y ice, every way, high an' low, an' some places black water, in-among; an' on'y the poor swiles bawlun all over, an' I standun amongst 'em.

"While I was lookun out, I sid a great icebarg (they calls 'em) a quarter of a mile away, or thereabouts, standun up,—one end a twenty fathom out o' water, an' about a forty fathom across, wi' hills like, an' houses,—an' then, jest as ef 'e was alive an' had tooked a notion in 'e'sself, seemunly, all of a sudden 'e rared up, an' turned over an' over, wi' a tarrible thunderun noise, an' comed right on, breakun everything an' throwun up great seas; 't was frightsome for a lone body away out among 'em! I stood an' looked at un, but then

107

agen I thowt I may jes' so well be goun to thick ice an' over Noofundland-ways a piece, so well as I could. So I said my bit of a prayer, an' told Un I could n' help myself; an' I made my confession how bad I'd been, an' I was sorry, an ef 'E 'd be so pitiful an' forgive me; an' ef I mus' loss my life, ef 'E 'd be so good as make me a good Christen first,—an' make they happy, in course.

"So then I started; an' first I goed to where my gaff was, by the mother-swile an' her whelp. There was swiles every two or three yards a'most, old uns an' young uns, all round everywhere; an' I feeled shamed in a manner: but I got my gaff, an' cleaned un, an' then, in God's name, I took the big swile, that was dead by its dead whelp, an' hauled it away, where the t' other poor things could n' si' me, an' I sculped[11] it, an' took the pelt;—for I thowt I'd wear un, now the poor dead thing did n' want to make oose of un no more,—an' partly becase 't was sech a lovun thing. An' so I set out, walkun this way for a spurt, an' then t' other way, keepun up mostly a Nor-norwest, so well as I could: sometimes away round th' open, an' more times round a lump of ice, an' more times, agen, off from one an' on to another, every minute. I did n' feel hungry, for I drinked fresh water off th' ice. No schooner! no schooner!

"Bumby the sun was goun down: 't was slow work feelun my way along, an' I did n' want to look about; but then agen I thowt God 'ad made it to be sid; an' so I come to, an' turned all round, an' looked; an' surely it seemed like another world, someway, 't was so beautiful,—yellow, an' different sorts o' red, like the sky itself in a manner, an' flashun like glass. So then it comed night; an' I thowt I should n' go to bed, an' I may forget my prayers, an' so I'd, mubbe, best say 'em right away; an' so I doned: 'Lighten our darkness,' and others we was oosed to say; an' it comed into my mind, the Lard said to Saint Peter, 'Why did n' 'ee have faith?' when there was nawthun on the water for un to go on; an' I had ice under foot,—'t was but frozen water, but 't was frozen,—an' I thanked Un.

"I could n' help thinkun o' Brigus an' them I'd laved in it, an' then I prayed for 'em; an' I could n' help cryun a'most; but then I give over agen, an' would n' think, ef I could help it; on'y tryun to say an odd psalm, all through singun-psalms an' other, for I knowed a many of 'em by singun wi' Patience, on'y now I cared more about 'em: I said that one,—

---

[11] Skinned.

'Sech as in ships an' brickle barks
    Into the seas descend,
Their merchantun, through fearful floods,
    To compass an' to end:
They men are force-put to behold
    The Lard's works, what they be;
An' in the dreadful deep the same
    Most marvellous they see.'

An' I said a many more (I can't be accountable how many I said), an' same uns many times, over: for I would keep on; an' 'ould sometimes sing 'em very loud in my poor way.

"A poor baste (a silver fox 'e was) comed an' looked at me; an' when I turned round, he walked away a piece, an' then 'e comed back, an' looked.

"So I found a high piece, wi' a wall of ice atop for shelter, ef it comed on to blow; an' so I stood, an' said, an' sung. I knowed well I was on'y driftun away.

"It was tarrible lonely in the night, when night comed; it's no use! 'T was tarrible lonely: but I 'ould n' think, ef I could help it; an' I prayed a bit, an' kep' up my psalms, an' varses out o' the Bible, I'd a-larned. I had n' a-prayed for sleep, but for wakun all night, an' there I was, standun.

"The moon was out agen, so bright; an' all the hills of ice shinun up to her; an' stars twinklun, so busy, all over; an' No'ther' Lights goun up wi' a faint, blaze, seemunly, from th' ice, an' meetun up aloft; an' sometimes a great groanun, an' more times tarrible loud shriekun! There was great white fields, an' great white hills, like countries, comun down to be destroyed; an' some great bargs a-goun faster, an' tearun through, breakun others to pieces; an' the groanun an' screechun,—ef all the dead that ever was, wi' their white clothès— But no!" said the stout fisherman, recalling himself from gazing, as he seemed to be, on the far-off ghastly scene, in memory.

"No!—an' thank 'E's marcy, I'm sittun by my own room. 'E tooked me off; but 't was a dreadful sight,—it's no use,—ef a body'd let 'e'sself think! I sid a great black bear, an' hard un growl; an' 't was feelun, like, to hear un so bold an' so stout, among all they dreadful things, an' bumby the time 'ould come when 'e could n' save 'e'sself, do what 'e woul'.

"An' more times 't was all still: on'y swiles bawlun, all over. Ef it had n' a-been for they poor swiles, how could I stan' it? Many's the one I'd a-ketched, daytime, an' talked to un, an' patted un on the head, as ef they'd a-been dogs by the door, like; an' they'd oose to shut their eyes, an' draw their poor foolish faces together. It seemed neighbor-like to have some live thing.

"So I kep' awake, sayun an' singun, an' it was n' very cold; an' so,— first thing I knowed, I started, an' there I was lyun in a heap; an' I must have been asleep, an' did n' know how 't was, nor how long I'd a-been so: an' some sort o' baste started away, an' 'e must have waked me up; I could n' rightly see what 't was, wi' sleepiness: an' then I hard a sound, sounded like breakers; an' that waked me fairly. 'T was like a lee-shore; an' 't was a comfort to think o' land, ef 't was on'y to be wrecked on itself: but I did n' go, an' I stood an' listened to un; an' now an' agen I'd walk a piece, back an' forth, an' back an' forth; an' so I passed a many, many longsome hours, seemunly, tull night goed down tarrible slowly, an' it comed up day o' t' other side: an' there was n' no land; nawthun but great mountains meltun an' breakun up, an' fields wastun away. I sid 't was a rollun barg made the noise like breakers; throwun up great seas o' both sides of un; no sight nor sign o' shore, nor ship, but dazun white,—enough to blind a body,—an' I knowed 't was all floatun away, over the say. Then I said my prayers, an' tooked a drink o' water, an' set out agen for Nor-norwest: 't was all I could do. Sometimes snow, an' more times fair agen; but no sign o' man's things, an' no sign o' land, on'y white ice an' black water; an' ef a schooner was n' into un a'ready, 't was n' likely they woul', for we was gettun furder an' furder away. Tired I was wi' goun, though I had n' walked more n' a twenty or thirty mile, mubbe, an' it all comun down so fast as I could go up, an' faster, an' never stoppun! 'T was a tarrible long journey up over the driftun ice, at sea! So, then I went on a high bit to wait tull all was done; I thowt 't would be last to melt, an' mubbe, I thowt 'e may capsize wi' me, when I did n' know (for I don' say I was stouthearted); an' I prayed Un to take care o' them I loved; an' the tears comed. Then I felt somethun tryun to turn me round like, an' it seemed as ef she was doun it, somehow, an' she seemed to be very nigh, somehow, an' I did n' look.

"After a bit, I got up to look out where most swiles was, for company, while I was livun: an' the first look struck me a'most like a bullet! There I sid a sail! 'T was a sail, an' 't was like heaven openun, an' God settun her down there. About three mile away she was, to nothe'ard, in th' Ice.

"I could ha' sid, at first look, what schooner 't was; but I did n' want to look hard at her. I kep' my peace, a spurt, an' then I runned an' bawled out, 'Glory be to God!' an' then I stopped, an' made proper thanks to Un. An' there she was, same as ef I'd a-walked off from her an hour ago! It felt so long as ef I'd been livun years, an' they would n' know me, sca'ce. Somehow, I did n' think I could come up wi' her.

"I started, in the name o' God, wi' all my might, an' went, an' went,— 't was a five mile, wi' goun round,—an' got her, thank God! 'T was n' the Baccaloue (I sid that long before), 't was t' other schooner, the Sparrow, repairun damages they'd got day before. So that kep' 'em there, an' I'd a-been took from one an' brought to t' other.

"I could n' do a hand's turn tull we got into the Bay agen,—I was so clear beat out. The Sparrow kep' her men, an' fotch home about thirty-eight hundred swiles, an' a poor man off th' Ice: but they, poor fellows, that I went out wi', never comed no more: an' I never went agen.

"I kep' the skin o' the poor baste, Sir: that's 'e on my cap."

When the planter had fairly finished his tale, it was a little while before I could teach my eyes to see the things about me in their places. The slow-going sail, outside, I at first saw as the schooner that brought away the lost man from the Ice; the green of the earth would not, at first, show itself through the white with which the fancy covered it; and at first I could not quite feel that the ground was fast under my feet. I even mistook one of my own men (the sight of whom was to warn me that I was wanted elsewhere) for one of the crew of the schooner Sparrow of a generation ago.

I got the tale and its scene gathered away, presently, inside my mind, and shook myself into a present association with surrounding things, and took my leave. I went away the more gratified that I had a chance of lifting my cap to a matron, dark-haired and comely (who, I was sure, at a glance, had once been the maiden of Benjie Westham's "troth-plight"), and receiving a handsome courtesy in return.

THE INVISIBLE PRINCESS

BY FRANCIS O'CONNOR

I could be "as tedious as a king," in analyzing those chivalrous instincts of masculine youth that lured me from college at nineteen, and away over the watery deserts of the sea; and, like Dogberry, "I could find in my heart to bestow it all of your worships." But since, like the auditor of that worthy, you do not want it, I will pass over the embarkation, which was tedious, over the sea-sickness, which was more tedious, over the home-sickness, over the monotonous duties assigned me, and the unvarying prospect of sea and sky, all so tedious that I grew as morose after a time as a travelling Englishman. Neither was coasting, with restricted liberty and much toil, amongst people whose language I could not speak, quite all that my fancy painted it,—although Genoa, Venice, the Bay of Naples,—crimsoned by Vesuvius, and canopied by an Italian sky,—and the storied scenes of Greece, all rich in beauties and historic associations, repaid many discomforts at the time and remain to me forever as treasures of memory the more precious for being dearly bought. But these, with the pleasures and displeasures of Constantinople,—the limit of our voyage,—I will pass over, to the midsummer eve when, with all the arrangements for our return voyage completed, we swung slowly out of the northern eddy of the Golden Horn into the clear blue Bosphorus.

Already the lengthening shadows of a thousand domes and minarets stretched across its waters, and glimpses of sunlight lay between them, like golden clasps linking continent to continent. Around us were ships and sailors from all parts of the habitable globe; while through shine and shadow flitted boats and caiques innumerable, and except where these, or the rising of a porpoise, or the dipping of a gull, broke the surface of the water, it lay as smooth as a mirror, reflecting its palace-guarded shores.

The men were lounging about the deck or leaning over the bulwarks, listening to a neighboring crew chanting their vespers, while we awaited the coming on board of our captain. Meanwhile the shadows crept up the Asian hills, till the last sombre answering smile to the sun's good-night faded from the cypress-trees above the graves of Scutari.

Beside me, long in silent admiration of the scene, stood my messmates, Fred Smith and Mike O'Hanlon,—two genuine specimens of Young New York, the first of whom disappointed love had driven to sea, whither also friendship and a reckless spirit of adventure had impelled the second. Behind us was one, a just impression of whom—if I could but convey it—would make what followed appear as possible to you as it did to us who were long his companions. I never knew to what country he belonged; for he spoke any language occasion called for, with the same apparent ease and fluency. He was far beyond the ordinary stature, yet it was only when you saw him in comparison with other men that you observed anything gigantic in his form. His hair was black, and hung in a smooth, heavy, even wave down to his massive jaw, which was always clean shaved, if indeed beard ever grew upon it. Neither could I guess his age; for though he was apparently in manhood's prime, it often appeared to me that the spirit I saw looking through his eyes must have been looking from them for a thousand years.

And how I used to exult in watching him deal with matter! He never took anything by the wrong end, nor failed to grasp a swinging rope or a flapping sail, nor miscalculated the effort necessary to the performance of whatever he undertook. He was silent, but not morose. Yet there was something in his measured tones and the gaze of his large gray eyes which Mike compared in their mingled effects to the charms of sight and sound that the victims of the rattlesnake's fascination are said to undergo. Whatever sensations they occasioned, men shrank from renewing them, and the frankest and boldest of the crew shunned occasions for addressing him. Stranger still, this feeling, instead of wearing off by the close companionship of our little bark, seemed to deepen and strengthen, until at length, except myself, no one spoke to him who could avoid it. Even the captain, when circumstances allowed him a choice, always directed his orders to another, though this man's duties were performed with the quiet promptness of a machine. If he was conscious of anything peculiar in the behavior of his companions toward him, he betrayed no indication of it. Such he was who stood listening, with an appearance of interest unusual in him, to our otherwise inconsequent chat.

"You are bidding a very silent adieu to the Genius of the East," I said.

"Yes," Fred answered, "it's her first actual revelation to me, but it's a glorious one."

"Let those who love to decipher illegible inscriptions, to contemplate a throttled centaur on a dilapidated frieze, or a carved acanthus on a fallen capital, grope over the Acropolis and invoke Athenian Pallas," said Mike; "but for me these painted seraglios and terraced, bower-canopied gardens, vocal with nightingales and seeming to impregnate the very air with the pleasures of desire, justify the decision of Paris. Hurrah for Asiatic Venus!"

"You are no true Christian knight," I said. "Your Rinaldos and Sir Guyons always waste your gardens of voluptuous delight, and wipe out their abominations."

"Yes," he retorted, "all but the abomination of desolation."

"But do you consider," said Fred, "how many sweet birds may be looking out through the bars of those bright lattice cages even now, who can follow neither their hearts' desires nor their souls' aspirations, but whom fate has degraded to be the slaves of some miserable old Blue Beard?"

"Why don't you sail in and rescue some of them?" said Mike mockingly. "Tell the old tyrant to his cerulean beard that he has too many strings to his bow, and he will undoubtedly spare a bow-string to twine around your manly neck. But I guess you had better, after all, leave the Fatimas to their fate. The barriers that fence them in from their hearts' desires and souls' aspirations here are not more real, if more palpable, than those that guard them in our land of boasted freedom; neither are they altogether secure from sale and barter there; and as for us outside barbarians, I'd as lief be shut out by palace walls from a beauty I can only imagine, as by custom still more insurmountable from beauty set visibly before me and enhanced with intellectual and social graces."

I cited the lady in the song, who says:—

> A tarry sailor I'll ne'er disdain,
> But always I will treat the same,

as proof that such exclusiveness was far from being the universal rule at home, and encouraged him to rival the "swabber, the boatswain and mate" for "Moll, Mag, Marion, and Margery."

"Or," said he, "like the jolly tar you quote, dismiss both your songs as 'scurvy tunes,' and, swigging at a black jack, say: Here's my comfort."

"I am not sure," said Fred bitterly, thinking of his own rejected suit, "that Stephano's philosophy is not the best for wretches like us."

"Yes," said Mike, "until after the Millennium. Then the march of civilization will be ended, and the ranks may be broken. Then soft hands and hard hands may clasp each other. Then rays from the purest and most refined souls may shine through bright eyes without being especially chilled for those whom a cold destiny makes especially needful of their heart-warming influences. Then you, poor as you are, may aspire to wed the daughter of a banker, and Joe or I may seek to satisfy the heart's desires of the Sultan's daughter, without Aladdin's lamp or Oberon's whistle."

Here our strange auditor came forward with a small tin whistle in his hand, and gravely presenting it to Fred, he advised him to try its note on the hard-hearted parent who opposed his happiness. In the deepening twilight, Fred and Mike, putting their heads together, read the following legend graven upon it:—

O whistle, and I'll come to you, my lad!

We all laughed outright, except the donor.

"This is not Oberon's whistle, at any rate," I said.

"No," he answered, "the inspiration of this is from Mammon, whose gates I understood shut Mr. Smith out from his true love. A single blast on it will, I dare say, open them wide enough to let him in."

"Then it's as good as money to you, Fred," said Mike.

"That's what our old boss used to tell us," answered Fred ruefully, "when he gave us orders on a neighboring grocery, in lieu of cash for our wages. But I must confess I have now, as I had then, a prejudice in favor of the circulating medium."

"If so, whistle for it at once," said the other.

Fred looked at him, and then at Mike and me, with a puzzled expression which seemed to ask: Is this a crazy freak, or an absurd, insulting joke?

115

"Now," said the object of this scrutiny, turning to me, "I have a talisman for you also, wherewith to entice the Sultan's daughter. It is a ruby of rare size and color, and therefore valuable. But the power of the spell it is said to possess remains to be tested. I give it to you because in you, at this moment, are fulfilled the conditions necessary to exercise this spell; which you do by simply taking the jewel in your hand thus, and saying,—

Come, O royal maiden, come to me this hour."

"And she'll come, of course," said Mike, bantering me in his turn. "Now hoist your signal and hail the daughter of the Grand Turk, and let Fred pipe for his princess at the same auspicious moment."

"Amen!" I said, holding up the gem till the moonbeams blushed red in it, and calling out with a strange, impulsive sense of power,—

"Come, O royal maiden, come to me this hour."

But no responsive tooting of the whistle echoed from the lips of Fred. I looked toward him for an explanation of the silence, and beheld him spitting out the fragments of the instrument, which had gone to pieces in his mouth.

"What's all this?" he exclaimed, unrolling a little scroll of paper that had been compressed within it, and holding it up to the light. "See here, Joe, what do you make of this?"

"A draft for ten thousand pounds sterling, on the Bank of England, duly signed and indorsed," I answered after scrutinizing it carefully.

We turned simultaneously for an explanation, but there was no one to give it.

"I always suspected who he was," said Mike, "but he's got no hold on me,—no claim to a bond signed with my blood. See, there he goes!"

I looked, and saw a boat shooting across the stream with a swiftness that argued some optical delusion. That unmistakable figure stood in the stern, urging it with a single scull, and as it disappeared in the confusion of boats and the darkness, a superstitious suspicion crept over me that he might be the person Mike suggested. Soon the captain came on board, and on learning the absence of the boat and its occupant, he expressed considerable anxiety and impatience. A breeze sprang up and began to curl the surface of the water, and

116

clouds obscured the moon. Then the wind freshened to a storm, and lifted the waves on the channel, and roared in the cypress forests above Pera and Scutari. Under the light sails already set, the ship tugged hard at her cable. Yet the boat did not return. The captain walked the deck nervously, and finally gave orders to weigh anchor, when just as our bark, freed to the wind and the current, sprang forward on her long voyage, the boat for which we were looking shot suddenly under the prow, and in an instant our mysterious comrade stepped in upon the deck from the bow-chains. As he did so, the light of the mate's lantern fell full upon him, and the scene it revealed will certainly never be forgotten by anyone who witnessed it.

There he stood, looming out from the tempestuous darkness more gigantic and terrible than ever, with the form of a beautiful girl, gorgeously clad and flashing with jewels, held easily and firmly by one encircling arm. His disengaged right hand was stained as if with blood, and spots of the same sanguinary hue were on his brow and his garments. The expression of his face was unmoved as usual.

For a moment he permitted the slippered feet of the trembling girl to rest upon the deck, though his arm still encompassed her shrinking form, and, while her great dark eyes, dilated with horror, like those of a captured bird, threw wild, eager glances to left and right, as if in search of any desperate refuge from the terrors that possessed her, he said in his usual quiet tones to the captain,—

"This is the passenger for whom I engaged the cabin. She will, by your leave, take possession of it at once." So saying, he led her gently forward and disappeared at the companion-way, conducted by the captain.

Every face on deck had grown pale, and every heart throbbed with the conviction that we had just beheld the consummation of a most desperate and bloody deed. It was evident the girl had been snatched suddenly from the harem of some palace, probably from the royal seraglio itself, off which we had been lying. And the horror depicted on her face, as well as the stains of blood on her abductor, told with what ruthless violence. Here then, I thought, in all human probability, was the royal maiden I had summoned; here was the wildest vagary of my imagination realized. But how different from the bright fancy was the woful reality!

Soon the captain returned on deck, pale and excited like the rest of us, and ordered a rash amount of sail to be set. The mate, a bluff, powerful man, swore an oath that we should first understand the meaning of what had just transpired.

"I know no more about it than you do," avowed the captain, "except that it's a piece of business very likely to bring all our heads to the block unless we show a clean pair of heels for it. So now avast jawing, and obey orders!"

"Never! boys," I said, "till we are assured of that girl's safety. What's done cannot be helped; but if she suffers further wrong in our midst, we ought all to be hanged as cowardly accessories to it."

"Dismiss your uneasiness in that regard," said a voice behind us, at whose sound there was a general start. "To keep her safe and inviolate is more my right and interest than yours, and it must therefore be my especial duty to do so; but if I fail in it, I care not though you make my life the forfeit, nor by what mode you exact it."

So saying, he took his place at the helm, a press of sail was set, and the ship fairly rent her way through the sea of Marmora before the tempest. But the ship, like all around, seemed to acknowledge his controlling power; and when I turned in with my watch, my sleep was undisturbed by any fear of wind or water, though it was full of troubled dreams. Now a lovely form in royal vesture beckoned to me from a lattice; anon the gleam of a lantern flickered across the terribly familiar face of a gnome, bearing out of a dark cavern an armful of the most precious jewels, which had a wild appealing in their light that puzzled me; while the roaring of the sea pervaded it all with a kind of dream harmony.

After a time, the fury of the tempest abated; but the ship still fled onward before strong gales, through those famous seas we had cruised so often in youthful fancy with the Greek and the Trojan, and the fear of pursuit ceased to haunt us.

Meanwhile we saw no more of our lovely passenger. Her strange guardian kept a watch beside her cabin door as vigilant as that of a sentinel at his post, or a saint before his shrine. His eye never swept the horizon behind us with an anxious gaze, as ours did, while we looked for the smoke of a pursuing steamer. Neither did it kindle at sight of the famous landmarks that measured our rapid course, each of which we hailed with delight as another harbinger of safety. He had ceased to perform the duties of a seaman, and devoted himself entirely to the care of the Invisible Princess, as we grew to call her. But though invisible to our eyes, hers was the pervading presence of our thoughts. Not a wave rocked the ship, not a cloud overshadowed it, not a morning breeze came fresh from the sea, or an evening breeze brought fragrance from the shore, but was thought of in some relation with her. There was none like her, we said, in the broad continents to right of us, to left of us, or before us; and we doubted if there was her like in the lands of enchantment we had left behind. Her wondrous beauty, the flashing of the jewels that encrusted her belt, and that seemed to gleam and sparkle all over her picturesque attire, the haunting look of those great, lustrous eyes, all the reminiscence of that eventful night,—how fondly we recurred to them again and again in the forecastle or the night-watch, and with what pleasure we recognized the first indications that her trance of terror had passed, and that she had resumed a living interest in the strange world around her.

First the open window of the cabin gave evidence that the balmy air and the pleasant shores we skirted were no longer indifferent to her; then came flitting glimpses of bright garments and brighter eyes quickly withdrawn from observation into the depths of the fairy grotto she inhabited; and finally, one beautiful moonlight evening, while most of the crew were on deck watching the lurid peak of Etna and the pavement of golden waves stretching toward it, and listening not to premonitions of Scylla or Charybdis, but to the song of the nightingales from the dim shore, or to tales of Enceladus and the Cyclops from Fred, and whimsical comments from Mike, she came hesitatingly forth, arousing an excitement and curiosity among us as intense as if she were a ghost arising from the tomb. Her dress was the same in which she had been brought among us, without addition of yashmak or veil of any kind,—excepting the mistiness of the moonlight,—to conceal her face, though there was a shy drawing down of the tasselled cap or turban she wore, that shadowed it somewhat.

I need hardly say how soon the glories of earth, sea, and sky, which we had been contemplating, shrank into mere accessories around that one central figure, as she stood gazing upon them through the shrouds and spars from our deck. But, notwithstanding the beauty of the scene and the hour, she did not hold her position long to enjoy them. She had, in appearing thus before strange men, evidently by a great effort, done that which she shrank from doing; but whether in obedience to her own will or to that of another, we

119

could not guess. The ice thus broken, however, she was the Invisible Princess no longer. Emboldened by two or three subsequent moonlight and twilight ventures, she at length came out in the sunset, and I doubt if the setting sun ever revealed a lovelier sight than greeted our eyes on that evening. A glance in the clear light satisfied us that the superhuman beauty we almost worshipped, and the splendor that seemed too lavish to be real, were no mere glamor of lamplight or moonlight, but surpassed in the reality all that our stunted, sceptical, Western imaginations, even stimulated as they were, had dared to anticipate.

I might attempt to describe her. I might tell you that her every limb and every feature seemed perfect in its form and its harmony with the others; that her complexion was a fresh, delicate bloom, without spot or blemish; that the innumerable braids of her long, black hair were ravishingly glossy and soft; that her great, dark eyes were bewilderingly bright and wise, and expressive of everything enchanting and good that eyes can express; that her smile,—but no! her smile was an expression of her individuality too subtle for words to catch; and without any power of revealing this individuality, this all that distinguished her from merely mortal woman and made her angelic, where is the use of attempting to describe her? Of her garments, by a recurrence to Lady Mary Wortley Montagu for the names of them, I could give you a description, from the golden-flowered, diamond-studded kerchief wreathed in her hair, to the yellow Cinderella slippers that covered her fairy feet. But the gauzy fabric that enfolded though it scarcely concealed her bosom, the vest of white damask stuff inwoven and fringed with gold and silver, the caftan, and the trousers of crimson embossed and embroidered with flowers of the same gorgeous materials, all were buttoned and guarded and overstrewn with jewels, while the broad belt that confined them was literally encrusted with diamonds and clasped by a magnificent bouquet of flowers wrought by the lapidary from diamonds, rubies, emeralds, sapphires, and pearls, so exquisitely that the artist showed a skill in them almost worthy of his materials.

From our ardent gaze the beautiful vision was soon withdrawn,—often to reappear, however, in the bright, calm weather that followed, each time with less of blushing and confusion in the beautiful face; and at length, some of us began to flatter ourselves, with a shy glance of interest and recognition for us in the luminous eyes.

On her strange companion, also, her presence shed a beam that lightened the darkness of our thoughts toward him. We marked the long, dark lashes of her eyes rising and falling, now trustingly, now fearingly, before that inscrutable countenance, as if her spirit wavered between a dream of terror and a contentful awaking. And many imagined that, as those dark eyes began to turn more lovingly and more longingly toward him, the strange brilliance of his own became imbued with their softness, while a faint auroral tinge seemed just ready to change his countenance from marble to flesh and blood.

Thus day after day we crept along the European coast, enjoying a dream of romance in which we could have gone on sailing contentedly forever, our only cause of uneasiness being that, at some of the numerous ports we touched, the magic presence on which the spell depended might go from us, as it came to us, without ceremony or warning, and leave us to cross the great ocean in the world of intolerable loneliness that would settle on the ship when she was gone. There was something like a patriotic aspiration in our desire to transplant this brightest of Eastern blossoms to diffuse its supreme beauty and sweetness in the West. And though we feared for her the stormy autumn passage of the Atlantic, a load was taken from every spirit when we left the Pillars of Hercules behind us and pointed our prow straight out across the cloud-bound ocean.

Just as we lost sight of land, we were attacked by a most violent storm, that buffeted us for many a day, during which we saw nothing of our fair passenger, and we learned that she was seriously ill. But never had invalid such a nurse as she. No one knew if he slept or ate, and no one was allowed to share his office, and no one obtruded on him the sorrow or sympathy which all felt in spite of our engrossing battle for life against the tempest. For though there was no change in his appearance or demeanor, all were conscious that a deep feeling stirred his heart. Even when we doubted if all our energies could preserve the vessel from being dashed back upon the coast we had just left, he gave us neither help nor heed, till in the final moment when we had given up all for lost, he seized the helm and shot us into shelter and safety behind the reef whereon we expected to go to pieces, through a channel which, in the calm that followed the storm, we found it difficult to retrace to the deep water, towing the ship with boats.

Again we got well out to sea, and were becalmed. For nearly a week, not a breeze had broken the surface of the ocean. Then another of those enchanting scenes we had feared to behold no more was presented to us. The beautiful invalid, assisted by her now inseparable companion, came upon the deck to watch the sunset. From her cheek the bloom of health was gone; but the look of wild dread with which hitherto she had never quite ceased to regard him who supported her was gone also, and in its place the large, dark eyes were filled by a glance of such indescribable gratitude and trust as only her eyes could express. He, for the first time, looked neither more nor less than a man. Her shrinking from our presence, too, had disappeared, and her look of recognition now was unmistakable and cordial. She had resumed her original garb, long disused as if to avoid remark at the ports we visited, and its glowing colors seemed to heighten the contrast between the pallid cheek and the long, dark lashes that drooped languidly over them, as, wearied at length by the unusual exertion, she sank heavily on her companion, and was rather borne than assisted back to the cabin.

During another week of breezeless autumn calm, this strange drama was re-enacted many times before us, with each time a deepening of the tragic shades that were gathering above it. But even after it became evident that the sweet evening air had no balm for the drooping girl, she loved to look out on the glories of the sunset, as if conscious that soon she should behold them no more forever. And when her strength no longer enabled her to walk, her nurse carried her out like a child in his arms.

But this also ceased after a time, and the hope that our transplanted blossom would ever flourish on a new soil had already faded from the bosom of the most sanguine among us, when one evening the guardian genius of the cabin beckoned to me from its portal. My entrance seemed to arouse the fair invalid, who was reclined upon a couch. The enchanting halo of her perfect beauty was unabated by disease; and she was surrounded by articles so rare, so costly, and in such profusion, as to force themselves upon my attention even in that first glance. A faint smile, and a recognition from those now too bright eyes, were my welcome. But they did not rest upon me long; for, as if by some fascination, those eyes seemed always turned toward him, or, if by chance he was beyond their reach, to the spot where they could first behold his return.

So this nursling of a palace, evidently dying out on the wide sea, with only rough men about her, had neither a word nor a look of reproach for the one who had dragged her forth to so wretched a fate. Even in her mind's wanderings, she seldom went back to former pomps or pleasures, and her tongue preferred rather to stumble through the rough and unfamiliar language in which of late she had been so terribly schooled, than to speak that of her youth. Once, when after a short absence her attendant returned to her side, she said,—

"My heart was trying to cross the waves that were between us, and oh! how it was tossed upon them—and it ached, and—and—" Then, giving a sigh of relief, she sank back, closed her eyes, and slumbered restfully.

He disposed of the lamp he had just lighted, and then, with an expression as inscrutable as ever, he stood looking down upon her.

While this scene was being enacted, I marked through the open portal of the cabin—in one of those strange distractions that occur to us amidst the most intense feelings of our lives—the stars above us growing brighter and brighter as the shades of the twilight deepened. Suddenly turning from the couch, he also, at a stride, stood in full view of those bright revelations of the darkness; but his eye sought them with no such abstracted regard as mine. Fixedly and sternly he seemed to be watching among them some portentous index of fate. Soon a change came over his countenance, and he resumed his place beside the scarcely breathing form. Then the fountains of the great deep within him were broken up, and the rushing torrent of its emotions shook his whole frame and convulsed his features. Stooping, he kissed the insensible girl passionately, again and again, and he would, I believe, have clasped her to his bosom if I, fearing for her the effects of his stormy transports, had not caught his arm. He needed no explanation of my interruption, neither was he startled or incensed by it, and he seemed more like one reluctantly obeying some sudden restraining impulse of his own than yielding to that of another.

"No," he said, "I must not cut short a single flicker of that bright spirit; the wondrously beautiful vessel that it glorifies will be cold clay soon enough! ashes from which no future Phœnix shall arise. O," he exclaimed, "this sacrifice is too great, too great! and for nothing! Even had she perished on the destined altar, an accepted sacrifice, it were too great! But I tore her from home and friends, and life itself, for this,—for nothing! O Destiny, thou art a subtle adversary, and infinite are thy devices for our overthrow! But I never reckoned on such an impediment as this heart-weakness."

Then approaching me, he laid a hand upon my shoulder, and said: "As the representative of the young, hopeful, living world she is about to leave, I called you here that you and she might look your last upon each other. Go now, and though your present emotion accords duly with the part I have assigned you, see that you do not play false to it hereafter by letting this woful event impress you with too deep or too lasting a sorrow."

Then to my Ideal, so strangely found and lost, I looked and murmured an adieu, and returned among my companions, reverenced as one who had been in a hallowed place.

It was the third evening after this, to me, memorable visit. Streaks of sable, with golden edges, barred the face of the setting sun, and promised to our hopes a change of weather. But this indication, important as it was after the long calm, was evidently not that which the whole ship's crew, officers and men, were now discussing,—as the converged attention of the scattered groups on the closed entrance of that silent, mysterious cabin testified.

"I know," said O'Hanlon, answering to an objection from some one in the group where he stood, "it would be like invading a sanctuary to intrude there; but the conviction sometimes comes over me that we have, all hands of us, from the captain down, acted in regard to this matter with the incapacity of men in a nightmare. Fear is a condition under which a true man should not breathe a moment without contest; and yet I know we have been all, more or less consciously, under its influence since this man came on board. Out upon us! I will, for myself at least, break through this dream of terror at once, by a tap at yonder door."

"It's the captain's place, not ours," said Smith, "to investigate this affair. Don't be too impulsive; you will get yourself into serious trouble."

"This is no matter of ordinary discipline," said the other; "the captain has a more substantial awe of this man than you or I,—and for more substantial reasons. He was aware of his wealth and power when we were not. How, without his knowledge, could the treasures worth a king's ransom, that adorn yonder coop, have been smuggled in or arranged there? But I am resolved, right or wrong, to do as I said."

124

I was questioning within myself whether to second him, when the door toward which he was advancing slowly opened, and once more the object of our discussion issued from it, and again in his arms was the beautiful form to which they had proved such a fatal resting-place. But none of the emotions of terror, trustfulness, or affection, which had alternately thrilled it in that position, did it now exhibit. The bright eyes were closed, the beautiful features settled in lasting repose. The glossy hair was daintily braided. The spotless garments were gracefully disposed. The jewels glittered conspicuously, as if relieved from the outvying lustre of her eyes. All, as in life, was pure and perfect; and as in life, so in death, she was still a revelation of transcendent beauty. A snowy winding-sheet, fringed with heavy coins, alternately of gold and of silver, and looped with silken cords on which bunches of the same precious metals hung as tassels, was so disposed that he could enfold her in it without laying her from his arms.

Stepping to the side of the vessel, he stood holding her thus in our view for a few moments; then, deftly and deliberately as usual, he wrapped the preciously weighted linen around her, stepped easily upon the bulwark, and with that perfect and deliberate poise so peculiar to him, and with his burden clasped firmly to his breast, he flung himself far clear of the ship, into the ocean, and was seen no more.

Thus vanished like a dream the romance of my life. Indeed, but for the lurid gleam of this strange jewel, a true type and testimony of it, I might yet grow to persuade myself it was a dream, so wondrous it becomes to me in memory.

THE ADVOCATE'S WEDDING-DAY

BY CATHERINE CROWE

Antoine de Chaulieu was the son of a poor gentleman of Normandy, with a long genealogy, a short rent-roll, and a large family. Jacques Rollet was the son of a brewer, who did not know who his grandfather was; but he had a long purse, and only two children. As these youths flourished in the early days of liberty, equality, and fraternity, and were near neighbors, they naturally hated each other. Their enmity commenced at school, where the delicate and refined De Chaulieu, being the only gentilhomme amongst the scholars, was the favorite of the master (who was a bit of an aristocrat in his heart), although he was about the worst dressed boy in the establishment, and never had a sou to spend; whilst Jacques Rollet, sturdy and rough, with smart clothes and plenty of money, got flogged six days in the week, ostensibly for being stupid and not learning his lessons,—which he did not,—but in reality for constantly quarrelling with and insulting De Chaulieu, who had not strength to cope with him.

When they left the academy, the feud continued in all its vigor, and was fostered by a thousand little circumstances, arising out of the state of the times, till a separation ensued, in consequence of an aunt of Antoine de Chaulieu's undertaking the expense of sending him to Paris to study the law, and of maintaining him there during the necessary period.

With the progress of events came some degree of reaction in favor of birth and nobility; and then Antoine, who had passed for the bar, began to hold up his head, and endeavor to push his fortunes; but fate seemed against him. He felt certain that if he possessed any gift in the world, it was that of eloquence, but he could get no cause to plead; and his aunt dying inopportunely, first his resources failed, and then his health. He had no sooner returned to his home than, to complicate his difficulties completely, he fell in love with Miss Natalie de Bellefonds, who had just returned from Paris, where she had been completing her education. To expatiate on the perfections of Mademoiselle Natalie would be a waste of ink and paper; it is sufficient to say that she really was a very charming girl, with a fortune which, though not large, would have been a most desirable addition to De Chaulieu, who had nothing. Neither was the fair Natalie indisposed to listen to his addresses; but her father could not be expected to countenance the suit of a gentleman, however well-born, who had not a ten-sous piece in the world, and whose prospects were a blank.

Whilst the ambitious and love-sick barrister was thus pining in unwelcome obscurity, his old acquaintance, Jacques Rollet, had been acquiring an undesirable notoriety. There was nothing really bad in Jacques; but having been bred up a democrat, with a hatred of the nobility, he could not easily accommodate his rough humor to treat them with civility when it was no longer safe to insult them. The liberties he allowed himself whenever circumstances brought him into contact with the higher classes of society, had led him into many scrapes, out of which his father's money had in one way or another released him; but that source of safety had now failed. Old Rollet, having been too busy with the affairs of the nation to attend to his business, had died insolvent, leaving his son with nothing but his own wits to help him out of future difficulties; and it was not long before their exercise was called for.

Claudine Rollet, his sister, who was a very pretty girl, had attracted the attention of Mademoiselle de Bellefonds's brother, Alphonse; and as he paid her more attention than from such a quarter was agreeable to Jacques, the young men had had more than one quarrel on the subject, on which occasion they had each, characteristically, given vent to their enmity, the one in contemptuous monosyllables, and the other in a volley of insulting words. But Claudine had another lover, more nearly of her own condition of life; this was Claperon, the deputy-governor of the Rouen jail, with whom she had made acquaintance during one or two compulsory visits paid by her brother to that functionary. Claudine, who was a bit of a coquette, though she did not altogether reject his suit, gave him little encouragement, so that, betwixt hopes and fears and doubts and jealousies, poor Claperon led a very uneasy kind of life.

Affairs had been for some time in this position, when, one fine morning, Alphonse de Bellefonds was not to be found in his chamber when his servant went to call him; neither had his bed been slept in. He had been observed to go out rather late on the previous evening, but whether he had returned nobody could tell. He had not appeared at supper, but that was too ordinary an event to awaken suspicion; and little alarm was excited till several hours had elapsed, when inquiries were instituted and a search commenced, which terminated in the discovery of his body, a good deal mangled, lying at the bottom of a pond which had belonged to the old brewery.

Before any investigation had been made, every person had jumped to the conclusion that the young man had been murdered, and that Jacques Rollet was the assassin. There was a strong presumption in favor of that opinion, which further perquisitions tended to confirm. Only the day before, Jacques had been heard to threaten Monsieur de Bellefonds with speedy vengeance. On the fatal evening, Alphonse and Claudine had been seen together in the neighborhood of the now dismantled brewery; and as Jacques, betwixt poverty and democracy, was in bad odor with the respectable part of society, it was not easy for him to bring witnesses to character or to prove an unexceptionable alibi. As for the Bellefonds and De Chaulieus, and the aristocracy in general, they entertained no doubt of his guilt; and finally, the magistrates coming to the same opinion, Jacques Rollet was committed for trial at the next assizes, and as a testimony of good-will, Antoine de Chaulieu was selected by the injured family to conduct the prosecution.

Here, at last, was the opportunity he had sighed for. So interesting a case, too, furnishing such ample occasion for passion, pathos, indignation! And how eminently fortunate that the speech which he set himself with ardor to prepare would be delivered in the presence of the father and brother of his mistress, and perhaps of the lady herself. The evidence against Jacques, it is true, was altogether presumptive; there was no proof whatever that he had committed the crime; and for his own part, he stoutly denied it. But Antoine de Chaulieu entertained no doubt of his guilt, and the speech he composed was certainly well calculated to carry that conviction into the bosom of others. It was of the highest importance to his own reputation that he should procure a verdict, and he confidently assured the afflicted and enraged family of the victim that their vengeance should be satisfied.

Under these circumstances, could anything be more unwelcome than a piece of intelligence that was privately conveyed to him late on the evening before the trial was to come on, which tended strongly to exculpate the prisoner, without indicating any other person as the criminal. Here was an opportunity lost. The first step of the ladder on which he was to rise to fame, fortune, and a wife was slipping from under his feet.

Of course so interesting a trial was anticipated with great eagerness by the public; the court was crowded with all the beauty and fashion of Rouen, and amongst the rest, doubly interesting in her mourning, sat the fair Natalie, accompanied by her family.

The young advocate's heart beat high; he felt himself inspired by the occasion; and although Jacques Rollet persisted in asserting his innocence, founding his defence chiefly on circumstances which were strongly corroborated by the information that had reached De Chaulieu the preceding evening, he was nevertheless convicted.

In spite of the very strong doubts he privately entertained respecting the justice of the verdict, even De Chaulieu himself, in the first flush of success, amidst a crowd of congratulating friends and the approving smiles of his mistress, felt gratified and happy; his speech had, for the time being, not only convinced others but himself; warmed with his own eloquence, he believed what he said. But when the glow was over, and he found himself alone, he did not feel so comfortable. A latent doubt of Rollet's guilt now pressed strongly on his mind, and he felt that the blood of the innocent would be on his head. It was true there was yet time to save the life of the prisoner; but to admit Jacques innocent, was to take the glory out of his own speech, and turn the sting of his argument against himself. Besides, if he produced the witness who had secretly given him the information, he should be self-condemned, for he could not conceal that he had been aware of the circumstance before the trial.

Matters having gone so far, therefore, it was necessary that Jacques Rollet should die; and so the affair took its course; and early one morning the guillotine was erected in the court-yard of the gaol, three criminals ascended the scaffold, and three heads fell into the basket, which were presently afterward, with the trunks that had been attached to them, buried in a corner of the cemetery.

Antoine de Chaulieu was now fairly started in his career, and his success was as rapid as the first step toward it had been tardy. He took a pretty apartment in the Hôtel Marbœuf, Rue Grange Batelière, and in a short time was looked upon as one of the most rising young advocates in Paris. His success in one line brought him success in another; he was soon a favorite in society, and an object of interest to speculating mothers; but his affections still adhered to his old love, Natalie de Bellefonds, whose family now gave their assent to the match,—at least prospectively,—a circumstance which furnished such additional incentive to his exertions, that in about two years from his first brilliant speech he was in a sufficiently flourishing condition to offer the young lady a suitable home.

In anticipation of the happy event, he engaged and furnished a suite of apartments in the Rue de Helder; and as it was necessary that the bride should come to Paris to provide her trousseau, it was agreed that the wedding should take place there, instead of at Bellefonds, as had been first projected,—an arrangement the more desirable, that a press of business rendered Monsieur de Chaulieu's absence from Paris inconvenient.

Brides and bridegrooms in France, except of the very high classes, are not much in the habit of making those honeymoon excursions so universal in this country. A day spent in visiting Versailles, or St. Cloud, or even the public places of the city, is generally all that precedes the settling down into the habits of daily life. In the present instance, St. Denis was selected, from the circumstance of Natalie's having a younger sister at school there, and also because she had a particular desire to see the Abbey.

The wedding was to take place on a Thursday; and on the Wednesday evening, having spent some hours most agreeably with Natalie, Antoine de Chaulieu returned to spend his last night in his bachelor apartments. His wardrobe and other small possessions had already been packed up, and sent to his future home; and there was nothing left in his room now but his new wedding suit, which he inspected with considerable satisfaction before he undressed and lay down to sleep.

Sleep, however, was somewhat slow to visit him, and the clock had struck one before he closed his eyes. When he opened them again, it was broad daylight, and his first thought was, had he overslept himself? He sat up in bed to look at the clock, which was exactly opposite; and as he did so, in the large mirror over the fireplace, he perceived a figure standing behind him. As the dilated eyes met his own, he saw it was the face of Jacques Rollet. Overcome with horror, he sank back on his pillow, and it was some minutes before he ventured to look again in that direction; when he did so, the figure had disappeared.

The sudden revulsion of feeling which such a vision was calculated to occasion in a man elate with joy may be conceived. For some time after the death of his former foe, he had been visited by not infrequent twinges of conscience; but of late, borne along by success and the hurry of Parisian life, these unpleasant remembrances had grown rarer, till at length they had faded away altogether. Nothing had been further from his thoughts than Jacques Rollet when he closed his eyes on the preceding night, or when he opened them to that sun which was to shine on what he expected to be the happiest day of his life. Where were the high-strung nerves now, the elastic frame, the bounding heart?

Heavily and slowly he arose from his bed, for it was time to do so; and with a trembling hand and quivering knees he went through the processes of the toilet, gashing his cheek with the razor, and spilling the water over his well-polished boots. When he was dressed, scarcely venturing to cast a glance in the mirror as he passed it, he quitted the room and descended the stairs, taking the key of the door with him, for the purpose of leaving it with the porter; the man, however, being absent, he laid it on the table in his lodge, and with a relaxed hand and languid step he proceeded to the carriage which quickly conveyed him to the church, where he was met by Natalie and her friends.

How difficult it was now to look happy, with that pallid face and extinguished eye!

"How pale you are! Has anything happened? You are surely ill?" were the exclamations that assailed him on all sides.

He tried to carry the thing off as well as he could, but he felt that the movements he would have wished to appear alert were only convulsive, and that the smiles with which he attempted to relax his features were but distorted grimaces. However, the church was not the place for further inquiries; and whilst Natalie gently pressed his hand in token of sympathy, they advanced to the altar, and the ceremony was performed; after which they stepped into the carriages waiting at the door, and drove to the apartments of Madame de Bellefonds, where an elegant déjeuner was prepared.

"What ails you, my dear husband?" inquired Natalie, as soon as they were alone.

"Nothing, love," he replied; "nothing, I assure you, but a restless night and a little overwork, in order that I might have to-day free to enjoy my happiness."

"Are you quite sure? Is there nothing else?"

"Nothing, indeed, and pray don't take notice of it; it only makes me worse."

Natalie was not deceived, but she saw that what he said was true,— notice made him worse; so she contented herself with observing him quietly and saying nothing; but as he felt she was observing him, she might almost better have spoken; words are often less embarrassing things than too curious eyes.

When they reached Madame de Bellefonds' he had the same sort of scrutiny to undergo, till he grew quite impatient under it, and betrayed a degree of temper altogether unusual with him. Then everybody looked astonished; some whispered their remarks, and others expressed them by their wondering eyes, till his brow knit, and his pallid cheeks became flushed with anger.

Neither could he divert attention by eating; his parched mouth would not allow him to swallow anything but liquids, of which he indulged in copious libations; and it was an exceeding relief to him when the carriage which was to convey them to St. Denis, being announced, furnished an excuse for hastily leaving the table.

Looking at his watch, he declared it was late; and Natalie, who saw how eager he was to be gone, threw her shawl over her shoulders, and bidding her friends good morning they hurried away.

It was a fine sunny day in June; and as they drove along the crowded boulevards and through the Porte St. Denis, the young bride and bridegroom, to avoid each other's eyes, affected to be gazing out of the windows; but when they reached that part of the road where there was nothing but trees on each side, they felt it necessary to draw in their heads, and make an attempt at conversation.

De Chaulieu put his arm round his wife's waist, and tried to rouse himself from his depression; but it had by this time so reacted upon her, that she could not respond to his efforts; and thus the conversation languished, till both felt glad when they reached their destination, which would, at all events, furnish them something to talk about.

Having quitted the carriage and ordered a dinner at the Hôtel de l'Abbaye, the young couple proceeded to visit Mademoiselle de Bellefonds, who was overjoyed to see her sister and new brother-in-law, and doubly so when she found that they had obtained permission to take her out to spend the afternoon with them.

As there is little to be seen at St. Denis but the Abbey, on quitting that part of it devoted to education, they proceeded to visit the church with its various objects of interest; and as De Chaulieu's thoughts were now forced into another direction, his cheerfulness began insensibly to return. Natalie looked so beautiful, too, and the affection betwixt the two young sisters was so pleasant to behold! And they spent a couple of hours wandering about with Hortense, who was almost as well informed as the Suisse, till the brazen doors were open which admitted them to the royal vault.

Satisfied at length with what they had seen, they began to think of returning to the inn, the more especially as De Chaulieu, who had not eaten a morsel of food since the previous evening, confessed to being hungry; so they directed their steps to the door, lingering here and there as they went to inspect a monument or a painting, when happening to turn his head aside to see if his wife, who had stopped to take a last look at the tomb of King Dagobert, was following, he beheld with horror the face of Jacques Rollet appearing from behind a column. At the same instant his wife joined him and took his arm, inquiring if he was not very much delighted with what he had seen. He attempted to say yes, but the word died upon his lips; and staggering out of the door, he alleged that a sudden faintness had overcome him.

They conducted him to the hotel, but Natalie now became seriously alarmed; and well she might. His complexion looked ghastly, his limbs shook, and his features bore an expression of indescribable horror and anguish. What could be the meaning of so extraordinary a change in the gay, witty, prosperous De Chaulieu, who, till that morning, seemed not to have a care in the world? For, plead illness as he might, she felt certain, from the expression of his features, that his sufferings were not of the body, but of the mind; and unable to imagine any reason for such extraordinary manifestations, of which she had never before seen a symptom, but a sudden aversion to herself, and regret for the step he had taken, her pride took the alarm, and, concealing the distress she really felt, she began to assume a haughty and reserved manner toward him, which he naturally interpreted into an evidence of anger and contempt.

The dinner was placed upon the table, but De Chaulieu's appetite, of which he had lately boasted, was quite gone; nor was his wife better able to eat. The young sister alone did justice to the repast; but although the bridegroom could not eat, he could swallow champagne in such copious draughts that erelong the terror and remorse which the apparition of Jacques Rollet had awakened in his breast were drowned in intoxication.

Amazed and indignant, poor Natalie sat silently observing this elect of her heart, till, overcome with disappointment and grief, she quitted the room with her sister, and retired to another apartment, where she gave free vent to her feelings in tears.

After passing a couple of hours in confidences and lamentations, they recollected that the hours of liberty, granted as an especial favor to Mademoiselle Hortense, had expired; but ashamed to exhibit her husband in his present condition to the eyes of strangers, Natalie prepared to reconduct her to the Maison Royal herself. Looking into the dining-room as they passed, they saw De Chaulieu lying on a sofa, fast asleep, in which state he continued when his wife returned. At length the driver of their carriage begged to know if monsieur and madame were ready to return to Paris, and it became necessary to arouse him.

The transitory effects of the champagne had now subsided; but when De Chaulieu recollected what had happened, nothing could exceed his shame and mortification. So engrossing, indeed, were these sensations, that they quite overpowered his previous ones, and, in his present vexation, he for the moment forgot his fears. He knelt at his wife's feet, begged her pardon a thousand times, swore that he adored her, and declared that the illness and the effect of the wine had been purely the consequences of fasting and overwork.

It was not the easiest thing in the world to reassure a woman whose pride, affection, and taste had been so severely wounded; but Natalie tried to believe, or to appear to do so, and a sort of reconciliation ensued, not quite sincere on the part of the wife, and very humbling on the part of the husband. Under these circumstances it was impossible that he should recover his spirits or facility of manner; his gayety was forced, his tenderness constrained; his heart was heavy within him; and ever and anon the source whence all this disappointment and woe had sprung would recur to his perplexed and tortured mind.

Thus mutually pained and distrustful, they returned to Paris, which they reached about nine o'clock. In spite of her depression, Natalie, who had not seen her new apartments, felt some curiosity about them, whilst De Chaulieu anticipated a triumph in exhibiting the elegant home he had prepared for her. With some alacrity, therefore, they stepped out of the carriage, the gates of the hotel were thrown open, the concierge rang the bell which announced to the servants that their master and mistress had arrived; and whilst these domestics appeared above, holding lights over the balusters, Natalie, followed by her husband, ascended the stairs.

But when they reached the landing-place of the first flight, they saw the figure of a man standing in a corner, as if to make way for them. The flash from above fell upon his face, and again Antoine de Chaulieu recognized the features of Jacques Rollet.

From the circumstance of his wife preceding him, the figure was not observed by De Chaulieu till he was lifting his foot to place it on the top stair: the sudden shock caused him to miss the step, and without uttering a sound, he fell back, and never stopped until he reached the stones at the bottom.

The screams of Natalie brought the concierge from below and the maids from above, and an attempt was made to raise the unfortunate man from the ground; but with cries of anguish he besought them to desist.

"Let me," he said, "die here. O God! what a dreadful vengeance is thine! Natalie, Natalie," he exclaimed to his wife, who was kneeling beside him, "to win fame, and fortune, and yourself, I committed a dreadful crime. With lying words I argued away the life of a fellow-creature, whom, whilst I uttered them, I half believed to be innocent; and now, when I have attained all I desired and reached the summit of my hopes, the Almighty has sent him back upon the earth to blast me with the sight. Three times this day—three times this day! Again! Again! Again!" And as he spoke, his wild and dilated eyes fixed themselves on one of the individuals that surrounded him.

"He is delirious," said they.

"No," said the stranger, "what he says is true enough, at least in part." And, bending over the expiring man, he added, "May Heaven forgive you, Antoine de Chaulieu! I am no apparition, but the veritable Jacques Rollet, who was saved by one who well knew my innocence. I may name him, for he is beyond the reach of the law now: it was Claperon, the jailer, who, in a fit of jealousy, had himself killed Alphonse de Bellefonds."

"But—but there were three," gasped Antoine.

"Yes, a miserable idiot, who had been so long in confinement for a murder that he was forgotten by the authorities, was substituted for me. At length I obtained, through the assistance of my sister, the position of concierge in the Hôtel Marbœuf, in the Rue Grange Bateliere. I entered on my new place yesterday evening, and was desired to awaken the gentleman on the third floor at seven o'clock. When I entered the room to do so, you were asleep; but before I had time to speak, you awoke, and I recognized your features in the glass. Knowing that I could not vindicate my innocence if you chose to seize me, I fled, and seeing an omnibus starting for St. Denis, I got on it with a vague idea of getting on to Calais and crossing the Channel to England. But having only a franc or two in my pocket, or indeed in the world, I did not know how to procure the means of going forward; and whilst I was lounging about the place, forming first one plan and then another, I saw you in the church, and, concluding that you were in pursuit of me, I thought the best way of eluding your vigilance was to make my way back to Paris as fast as I could; so I set off instantly, and walked all the way; but having no money to pay my night's lodging, I came here to borrow a couple of livres of my sister Claudine, who is a brodeuse and resides au cinquième."

"Thank Heaven!" exclaimed the dying man, "that sin is off my soul. Natalie, dear wife, farewell! Forgive—forgive all."

These were the last words he uttered; the priest, who had been summoned in haste, held up the cross before his failing sight; a few strong convulsions shook the poor bruised and mangled frame; and then all was still.

THE BIRTHMARK

BY NATHANIEL HAWTHORNE

In the latter part of the last century there lived a man of science, an eminent proficient in every branch of natural philosophy, who not long before our story opens had made experience of a spiritual affinity more attractive than any chemical one. He had left his laboratory to the care of an assistant, cleared his fine countenance from the furnace-smoke, washed the stain of acids from his fingers, and persuaded a beautiful woman to become his wife. In those days, when the comparatively recent discovery of electricity and other kindred mysteries of Nature seemed to open paths into the region of miracle, it was not unusual for the love of science to rival the love of woman in its depth and absorbing energy. The higher intellect, the imagination, the spirit, and even the heart might all find their congenial aliment in pursuits which, as some of their ardent votaries believed, would ascend from one step of powerful intelligence to another, until the philosopher should lay his hand on the secret of creative force and perhaps make new worlds for himself. We know not whether Aylmer possessed this degree of faith in man's ultimate control over nature. He had devoted himself, however, too unreservedly to scientific studies ever to be weaned from them by any second passion. His love for his young wife might prove the stronger of the two; but it could only be by intertwining itself with his love of science and uniting the strength of the latter to its own.

Such a union accordingly took place, and was attended with truly remarkable consequences and a deeply impressive moral. One day, very soon after their marriage, Aylmer sat gazing at his wife with a trouble in his countenance that grew stronger until he spoke.

"Georgiana," said he, "has it never occurred to you that the mark upon your cheek might be removed?"

"No, indeed," said she, smiling; but, perceiving the seriousness of his manner, she blushed deeply. "To tell you the truth, it has been so often called a charm, that I was simple enough to imagine it might be so."

"Ah, upon another face perhaps it might," replied her husband; "but never on yours. No, dearest Georgiana, you came so nearly perfect from the hand of Nature that this slightest possible defect, which we hesitate whether to term a defect or a beauty, shocks me, as being the visible mark of earthly imperfection."

"Shocks you, my husband!" cried Georgiana, deeply hurt; at first reddening with momentary anger, but then bursting into tears. "Then why did you take me from my mother's side? You cannot love what shocks you!"

To explain this conversation, it must be mentioned that in the centre of Georgiana's left cheek there was a singular mark, deeply interwoven, as it were, with the texture and substance of her face. In the usual state of her complexion,—a healthy though delicate bloom,—the mark wore a tint of deeper crimson, which imperfectly defined its shape amid the surrounding rosiness. When she blushed it gradually became more indistinct, and finally vanished amid the triumphant rush of blood that bathed the whole cheek with its brilliant glow. But if any shifting emotion caused her to turn pale there was the mark again, a crimson stain upon the snow, in what Aylmer sometimes deemed an almost fearful distinctness. Its shape bore not a little similarity to the human hand, though of the smallest pygmy size. Georgiana's lovers were wont to say that some fairy at her birth hour had laid her tiny hand upon the infant's cheek, and left this impress there in token of the magic endowments that were to give her such sway over all hearts. Many a desperate swain would have risked life for the privilege of pressing his lips to the mysterious hand. It must not be concealed, however, that the impression wrought by this fairy sign-manual varied exceedingly according to the difference of temperament in the beholders. Some fastidious persons—but they were exclusively of her own sex— affirmed that the bloody hand, as they chose to call it, quite destroyed the effect of Georgiana's beauty and rendered her countenance even hideous. But it would be as reasonable to say that one of those small blue stains which sometimes occur in the purest statuary marble would convert the Eve of Powers to a monster. Masculine observers, if the birthmark did not heighten their admiration, contented themselves with wishing it away, that the world might possess one living specimen of ideal loveliness without the semblance of a flaw. After his marriage—for he thought little or nothing of the matter before—Aylmer discovered that this was the case with himself.

Had she been less beautiful,—if Envy's self could have found aught else to sneer at,—he might have felt his affection heightened by the prettiness of this mimic hand, now vaguely portrayed, now lost, now stealing forth again and glimmering to and fro with every pulse of emotion that throbbed within her heart; but, seeing her otherwise so perfect, he found this one defect grow more and more intolerable with every moment of their united lives. It was the fatal flaw of humanity which Nature, in one shape or another, stamps ineffaceably on all her productions, either to imply that they are temporary and finite, or that their perfection must be wrought by toil and pain. The crimson hand expressed the ineludible gripe in which mortality clutches the highest and purest of earthly mould, degrading them into kindred with the lowest, and even with the very brutes, like whom their visible frames return to dust. In this manner, selecting it as the symbol of his wife's liability to sin, sorrow, decay, and death, Aylmer's sombre imagination was not long in rendering the birthmark a frightful object, causing him more trouble and horror than ever Georgiana's beauty, whether of soul or sense, had given him delight.

At all the seasons which should have been their happiest he invariably, and without intending it, nay, in spite of a purpose to the contrary, reverted to this one disastrous topic. Trifling as it at first appeared, it so connected itself with innumerable trains of thought and modes of feeling that it became the central point of all. With the morning twilight Aylmer opened his eyes upon his wife's face and recognized the symbol of imperfection; and when they sat together at the evening hearth his eyes wandered stealthily to her cheek, and beheld, flickering with the blaze of the wood fire, the spectral hand that wrote mortality where he would fain have worshipped. Georgiana soon learned to shudder at his gaze. It needed but a glance with the peculiar expression that his face often wore to change the roses of her cheek into a deathlike paleness, amid which the crimson hand was brought strongly out, like a bas-relief of ruby on the whitest marble.

Late one night, when the lights were growing dim so as hardly to betray the stain on the poor wife's cheek, she herself, for the first time, voluntarily took up the subject.

"Do you remember, my dear Aylmer," said she, with a feeble attempt at a smile, "have you any recollection, of a dream last night about this odious hand?"

"None! none whatever!" replied Aylmer, starting; but then he added, in a dry, cold tone, affected for the sake of concealing the real depth of his emotion, "I might well dream of it; for, before I fell asleep, it had taken a pretty firm hold of my fancy."

"And you did dream of it?" continued Georgiana, hastily; for she dreaded lest a gush of tears should interrupt what she had to say. "A terrible dream! I wonder that you can forget it. Is it possible to forget this one expression?—'It is in her heart now; we must have it out!' Reflect, my husband; for by all means I would have you recall that dream."

The mind is in a sad state when Sleep, the all-involving, cannot confine her spectres within the dim region of her sway, but suffers them to break forth affrighting this actual life with secrets that perchance belong to a deeper one. Aylmer now remembered his dream. He had fancied himself with his servant Aminadab attempting an operation for the removal of the birthmark; but the deeper went the knife, the deeper sank the hand, until at length its tiny grasp appeared to have caught hold of Georgiana's heart; whence, however, her husband was inexorably resolved to cut or wrench it away.

When the dream had shaped itself perfectly in his memory, Aylmer sat in his wife's presence with a guilty feeling. Truth often finds its way to the mind close muffled in robes of sleep, and then speaks with uncompromising directness of matters in regard to which we practise an unconscious self-deception during our waking moments. Until now he had not been aware of the tyrannizing influence acquired by one idea over his mind, and of the lengths which he might find in his heart to go for the sake of giving himself peace.

"Aylmer," resumed Georgiana, solemnly, "I know not what may be the cost to both of us to rid me of this fatal birthmark. Perhaps its removal may cause cureless deformity; or it may be the stain goes as deep as life itself. Again: do we know that there is a possibility, on any terms, of unclasping the firm gripe of this little hand which was laid upon me before I came into the world?"

"Dearest Georgiana, I have spent much thought upon the subject," hastily interrupted Aylmer. "I am convinced of the perfect practicability of its removal."

"If there be the remotest possibility of it," continued Georgiana, "let the attempt be made, at whatever risk. Danger is nothing to me; for life, while this hateful mark makes me the object of your horror and disgust,—life is a burden which I would fling down with joy. Either remove this dreadful hand, or take my wretched life! You have deep science. All the world bears witness of it. You have achieved great wonders. Cannot you remove this little, little mark, which I cover with the tips of two small fingers? Is this beyond your power, for the sake of your own peace, and to save your poor wife from madness?"

"Noblest, dearest, tenderest wife," cried Aylmer, rapturously, "doubt not my power. I have already given this matter the deepest thought,—thought which might almost have enlightened me to create a being less perfect than yourself. Georgiana, you have led me deeper than ever into the heart of science. I feel myself fully competent to render this dear cheek as faultless as its fellow; and then, most beloved, what will be my triumph when I shall have corrected what Nature left imperfect in her fairest work! Even Pygmalion, when his sculptured woman assumed life, felt not greater ecstasy than mine will be."

"It is resolved, then," said Georgiana, faintly smiling. "And, Aylmer, spare me not, though you should find the birthmark take refuge in my heart at last."

Her husband tenderly kissed her cheek,—her right cheek,—not that which bore the impress of the crimson hand.

The next day Aylmer apprised his wife of a plan that he had formed whereby he might have opportunity for the intense thought and constant watchfulness which the proposed operation would require; while Georgiana, likewise, would enjoy the perfect repose essential to its success. They were to seclude themselves in the extensive apartments occupied by Aylmer as a laboratory, and where, during his toilsome youth, he had made discoveries in the elemental powers of Nature that had roused the admiration of all the learned societies in Europe. Seated calmly in this laboratory, the pale philosopher had investigated the secrets of the highest cloud region and of the profoundest mines; he had satisfied himself of the causes that kindled and kept alive the fires of the volcano; and had explained the mystery of fountains, and how it is that they gush forth, some so bright and pure, and others with such rich medicinal virtues, from the dark bosom of the earth. Here, too, at an earlier period, he had studied the wonders of the human frame, and attempted to fathom the very process by which Nature assimilates all her precious influences from earth and air, and from the spiritual world, to create and foster man, her masterpiece. The latter pursuit, however, Aylmer had long laid aside in unwilling recognition of the truth—against which all seekers sooner or later stumble—that our great creative Mother, while she amuses us with apparently working in the broadest sunshine, is yet severely careful to keep her own secrets, and, in spite of her pretended openness, shows us nothing but results. She permits us, indeed, to mar, but seldom to mend, and, like a jealous patentee, on no account to make. Now, however, Aylmer resumed these half-forgotten investigations; not, of course, with such hopes or wishes as first suggested them; but because they involved much physiological truth and lay in the path of his proposed scheme for the treatment of Georgiana.

As he led her over the threshold of the laboratory, Georgiana was cold and tremulous. Aylmer looked cheerfully into her face, with intent to reassure her, but was so startled with the intense glow of the birthmark upon the whiteness of her cheek that he could not restrain a strong convulsive shudder. His wife fainted.

"Aminadab! Aminadab!" shouted Aylmer, stamping violently on the floor.

Forthwith there issued from an inner apartment a man of low stature, but bulky frame, with shaggy hair hanging about his visage, which was grimed with the vapors of the furnace. This personage had been Aylmer's under-worker during his whole scientific career, and was admirably fitted for that office by his great mechanical readiness, and the skill with which, while incapable of comprehending a single principle, he executed all the details of his master's experiments. With his vast strength, his shaggy hair, his smoky aspect, and the indescribable earthiness that incrusted him, he seemed to represent man's physical nature; while Aylmer's slender figure and pale, intellectual face were no less apt a type of the spiritual element.

"Throw open the door of the boudoir, Aminadab," said Aylmer, "and burn a pastil."

"Yes, master," answered Aminadab, looking intently at the lifeless form of Georgiana; and then he muttered to himself, "If she were my wife, I'd never part with that birthmark."

When Georgiana recovered consciousness she found herself

breathing an atmosphere of penetrating fragrance, the gentle potency of which had recalled her from her deathlike faintness. The scene around her looked like enchantment. Aylmer had converted those smoky, dingy, sombre rooms, where he had spent his brightest years in recondite pursuits, into a series of beautiful apartments not unfit to be the secluded abode of a lovely woman. The walls were hung with gorgeous curtains, which imparted the combination of grandeur and grace that no other species of adornment can achieve; and, as they fell from the ceiling to the floor, their rich and ponderous folds, concealing all angles and straight lines, appeared to shut in the scene from infinite space. For aught Georgiana knew, it might be a pavilion among the clouds. And Aylmer, excluding the sunshine, which would have interfered with his chemical processes, had supplied its place with perfumed lamps, emitting flames of various hue, but all uniting in a soft, impurpled radiance. He now knelt by his wife's side, watching her earnestly, but without alarm; for he was confident in his science, and felt that he could draw a magic circle round her within which no evil might intrude.

"Where am I? Ah, I remember," said Georgiana, faintly; and she placed her hand over her cheek to hide the terrible mark from her husband's eyes.

"Fear not, dearest!" exclaimed he. "Do not shrink from me! Believe me, Georgiana, I even rejoice in this single imperfection, since it will be such a rapture to remove it."

"O, spare me!" sadly replied his wife. "Pray do not look at it again. I never can forget that convulsive shudder."

In order to soothe Georgiana, and, as it were, to release her mind from the burden of actual things, Aylmer now put in practice some of the light and playful secrets which science had taught him among its profounder lore. Airy figures, absolutely bodiless ideas, and forms of unsubstantial beauty came and danced before her, imprinting their momentary footsteps on beams of light. Though she had some indistinct idea of the method of these optical phenomena, still the illusion was almost perfect enough to warrant the belief that her husband possessed sway over the spiritual world. Then again, when she felt a wish to look forth from her seclusion, immediately, as if her thoughts were answered, the procession of external existence flitted across a screen. The scenery and the figures of actual life were perfectly represented, but with that

143

bewitching yet indescribable difference which always makes a picture, an image, or a shadow so much more attractive than the original. When wearied of this, Aylmer bade her cast her eyes upon a vessel containing a quantity of earth. She did so, with little interest at first; but was soon startled to perceive the germ of a plant shooting upward from the soil. Then came the slender stalk; the leaves gradually unfolded themselves; and amid them was a perfect and lovely flower.

"It is magical!" cried Georgiana. "I dare not touch it."

"Nay, pluck it," answered Aylmer,—"pluck it, and inhale its brief perfume while you may. The flower will wither in a few moments and leave nothing save its brown seed-vessels; but thence may be perpetuated a race as ephemeral as itself."

But Georgiana had no sooner touched the flower than the whole plant suffered a blight, its leaves turning coal-black as if by the agency of fire.

"There was too powerful a stimulus," said Aylmer, thoughtfully.

To make up for this abortive experiment, he proposed to take her portrait by a scientific process of his own invention. It was to be effected by rays of light striking upon a polished plate of metal. Georgiana assented; but, on looking at the result, was affrighted to find the features of the portrait blurred and indefinable; while the minute figure of a hand appeared where the cheek should have been. Aylmer snatched the metallic plate and threw it into a jar of corrosive acid.

Soon, however, he forgot these mortifying failures. In the intervals of study and chemical experiment he came to her flushed and exhausted, but seemed invigorated by her presence, and spoke in glowing language of the resources of his art. He gave a history of the long dynasty of the alchemists, who spent so many ages in quest of the universal solvent by which the golden principle might be elicited from all things vile and base. Aylmer appeared to believe that, by the plainest scientific logic, it was altogether within the limits of possibility to discover this long-sought medium. "But," he added, "a philosopher who should go deep enough to acquire the power would attain too lofty a wisdom to stoop to the exercise of it." Not less singular were his opinions in regard to the elixir vitæ. He more than intimated that it was at his option to concoct a liquid that should prolong life for years, perhaps interminably; but that it would produce a discord in Nature which all the world, and chiefly the quaffer of the immortal nostrum, would find cause to curse.

"Aylmer, are you in earnest?" asked Georgiana, looking at him with amazement and fear. "It is terrible to possess such power, or even to dream of possessing it."

"O, do not tremble, my love!" said her husband. "I would not wrong either you or myself by working such inharmonious effects upon our lives; but I would have you consider how trifling, in comparison, is the skill requisite to remove this little hand."

At the mention of the birthmark, Georgiana, as usual, shrank as if a red-hot iron had touched her cheek.

Again Aylmer applied himself to his labors. She could hear his voice in the distant furnace-room giving directions to Aminadab, whose harsh, uncouth, misshapen tones were audible in response, more like the grunt or growl of a brute than human speech. After hours of absence, Aylmer reappeared and proposed that she should now examine his cabinet of chemical products and natural treasures of the earth. Among the former he showed her a small vial, in which, he remarked, was contained a gentle yet most powerful fragrance, capable of impregnating all the breezes that blow across a kingdom. They were of inestimable value, the contents of that little vial; and, as he said so, he threw some of the perfume into the air and filled the room with piercing and invigorating delight.

"And what is this?" asked Georgiana, pointing to a small crystal globe containing a gold-colored liquid. "It is so beautiful to the eye that I could imagine it the elixir of life."

"In one sense it is," replied Aylmer; "or rather, the elixir of immortality. It is the most precious poison that ever was concocted in this world. By its aid I could apportion the lifetime of any mortal at whom you might point your finger. The strength of the dose would determine whether he were to linger out years, or drop dead in the midst of a breath. No king on his guarded throne could keep his life if I, in my private station, should deem that the welfare of millions justified me in depriving him of it."

"Why do you keep such a terrific drug?" inquired Georgiana in horror.

"Do not mistrust me, dearest," said her husband, smiling; "its virtuous potency is yet greater than its harmful one. But see! here is a powerful cosmetic. With a few drops of this in a vase of water, freckles may be washed away as easily as the hands are cleansed. A stronger infusion would take the blood out of the cheek, and leave the rosiest beauty a pale ghost."

"Is it with this lotion that you intend to bathe my cheek?" asked Georgiana, anxiously.

"O, no," hastily replied her husband; "this is merely superficial. Your case demands a remedy that shall go deeper."

In his interviews with Georgiana, Aylmer generally made minute inquiries as to her sensations, and whether the confinement of the rooms and the temperature of the atmosphere agreed with her. These questions had such a particular drift that Georgiana began to conjecture that she was already subjected to certain physical influences, either breathed in with the fragrant air or taken with her food. She fancied likewise, but it might be altogether fancy, that there was a stirring up of her system,—a strange, indefinite sensation creeping through her veins, and tingling, half painfully, half pleasurably, at her heart. Still, whenever she dared to look into the mirror, there she beheld herself pale as a white rose and with the crimson birthmark stamped upon her cheek. Not even Aylmer now hated it so much as she.

To dispel the tedium of the hours which her husband found it necessary to devote to the processes of combination and analysis, Georgiana turned over the volumes of his scientific library. In many dark old tomes she met with chapters full of romance and poetry. They were the works of the philosophers of the Middle Ages, such as Albertus Magnus, Cornelius Agrippa, Paracelsus, and the famous friar who created the prophetic Brazen Head. All these antique naturalists stood in advance of their centuries, yet were imbued with some of their credulity, and therefore were believed, and perhaps imagined themselves to have acquired from the investigation of nature a power above nature, and from physics a sway over the spiritual world. Hardly less curious and imaginative were the early volumes of the Transactions of the Royal Society, in which the members, knowing little of the limits of natural possibility, were continually recording wonders or proposing methods whereby wonders might be wrought.

146

But, to Georgiana, the most engrossing volume was a large folio from her husband's own hand, in which he had recorded every experiment of his scientific career, its original aim, the methods adopted for its development, and its final success or failure, with the circumstances to which either event was attributable. The book, in truth, was both the history and emblem of his ardent, ambitious, imaginative, yet practical and laborious life. He handled physical details as if there were nothing beyond them; yet spiritualized them all, and redeemed himself from materialism by his strong and eager aspiration toward the infinite. In his grasp the veriest clod of earth assumed a soul. Georgiana, as she read, reverenced Aylmer and loved him more profoundly than ever, but with a less entire dependence on his judgment than heretofore. Much as he had accomplished, she could not but observe that his most splendid successes were almost invariably failures, if compared with the ideal at which he aimed. His brightest diamonds were the merest pebbles, and felt to be so by himself, in comparison with the inestimable gems which lay hidden beyond his reach. The volume, rich with achievements that had won renown for its author, was yet as melancholy a record as ever mortal hand had penned. It was the sad confession and continual exemplification of the shortcomings of the composite man, the spirit burdened with clay and working in matter, and of the despair that assails the higher nature at finding itself so miserably thwarted by the earthly part. Perhaps every man of genius, in whatever sphere, might recognize the image of his own experience in Aylmer's journal.

So deeply did these reflections affect Georgiana, that she laid her face upon the open volume and burst into tears. In this situation she was found by her husband.

"It is dangerous to read in a sorcerer's books," said he with a smile, though his countenance was uneasy and displeased. "Georgiana, there are pages in that volume which I can scarcely glance over and keep my senses. Take heed lest it prove as detrimental to you."

"It has made me worship you more than ever," said she.

"Ah, wait for this one success," rejoined he, "then worship me if you will. I shall deem myself hardly unworthy of it. But come, I have sought you for the luxury of your voice. Sing to me, dearest."

So she poured out the liquid music of her voice to quench the thirst of his spirit. He then took his leave with a boyish exuberance of gayety, assuring her that her seclusion would endure but a little longer, and that the result was already certain. Scarcely had he departed when Georgiana felt irresistibly impelled to follow him. She had forgotten to inform Aylmer of a symptom which for two or three hours past had begun to excite her attention. It was a sensation in the fatal birthmark, not painful, but which induced a restlessness throughout her system. Hastening after her husband, she intruded for the first time into the laboratory.

The first thing that struck her eye was the furnace, that hot and feverish worker, with the intense glow of its fire, which by the quantities of soot clustered above it seemed to have been burning for ages. There was a distilling apparatus in full operation. Around the room were retorts, tubes, cylinders, crucibles, and other apparatus of chemical research. An electrical machine stood ready for immediate use. The atmosphere felt oppressively close, and was tainted with gaseous odors which had been tormented forth by the processes of science. The severe and homely simplicity of the apartment, with its naked walls and brick pavement, looked strange, accustomed as Georgiana had become to the fantastic elegance of her boudoir. But what chiefly, indeed almost solely, drew her attention, was the aspect of Aylmer himself.

He was pale as death, anxious and absorbed, and hung over the furnace as if it depended upon his utmost watchfulness whether the liquid which it was distilling should be the draught of immortal happiness or misery. How different from the sanguine and joyous mien that he had assumed for Georgiana's encouragement!

"Carefully now, Aminadab; carefully, thou human machine; carefully, thou man of clay," muttered Aylmer, more to himself than his assistant. "Now, if there be a thought too much or too little, it is all over."

"Ho! ho!" mumbled Aminadab. "Look, master! look!"

Aylmer raised his eyes hastily, and at first reddened, then grew paler than ever, on beholding Georgiana. He rushed towards her and seized her arm with a gripe that left the print of his fingers upon it.

"Why do you come hither? Have you no trust in your husband?" cried he, impetuously. "Would you throw the blight of that fatal birthmark over my labors? It is not well done. Go, prying woman! go!"

148

"Nay, Aylmer," said Georgiana with the firmness of which she possessed no stinted endowment, "it is not you that have a right to complain. You mistrust your wife; you have concealed the anxiety with which you watch the development of this experiment. Think not so unworthily of me, my husband. Tell me all the risk we run, and fear not that I shall shrink; for my share in it is far less than your own."

"No, no, Georgiana!" said Aylmer, impatiently; "it must not be."

"I submit," replied she, calmly. "And, Aylmer, I shall quaff whatever draught you bring me; but it will be on the same principle that would induce me to take a dose of poison if offered by your hand."

"My noble wife," said Aylmer, deeply moved, "I knew not the height and depth of your nature until now. Nothing shall be concealed. Know, then, that this crimson hand, superficial as it seems, has clutched its grasp into your being with a strength of which I had no previous conception. I have already administered agents powerful enough to do aught except to change your entire physical system. Only one thing remains to be tried. If that fail us we are ruined."

"Why did you hesitate to tell me this?" asked she.

"Because, Georgiana," said Aylmer, in a low voice, "there is danger."

"Danger? There is but one danger,—that this horrible stigma shall be left upon my cheek!" cried Georgiana. "Remove it, remove it, whatever be the cost, or we shall both go mad!"

"Heaven knows your words are too true," said Aylmer, sadly. "And now, dearest, return to your boudoir. In a little while all will be tested."

He conducted her back and took leave of her with a solemn tenderness which spoke far more than his words how much was now at stake. After his departure Georgiana became rapt in musings. She considered the character of Aylmer, and did it completer justice than at any previous moment. Her heart exulted, while it trembled, at his honorable love,—so pure and lofty that it would accept nothing less than perfection nor miserably make itself contented with an earthlier nature than he had dreamed of. She felt how much more precious was such a sentiment than that meaner kind which would have borne with the imperfection for her sake, and have been guilty of treason to holy love by degrading its perfect idea to the level of the actual; and with her whole spirit she prayed that, for a single moment, she might satisfy his highest and deepest conception. Longer than one moment she well knew it could not be; for his spirit was ever on the march, ever ascending, and each instant required something that was beyond the scope of the instant before.

The sound of her husband's footsteps aroused her. He bore a crystal goblet containing a liquor colorless as water, but bright enough to be the draught of immortality. Aylmer was pale; but it seemed rather the consequence of a highly wrought state of mind and tension of spirit than of fear or doubt.

"The concoction of the draught has been perfect," said he, in answer to Georgiana's look. "Unless all my science have deceived me, it cannot fail."

"Save on your account, my dearest Aylmer," observed his wife, "I might wish to put off this birthmark of mortality by relinquishing mortality itself in preference to any other mode. Life is but a sad possession to those who have attained precisely the degree of moral advancement at which I stand. Were I weaker and blinder, it might be happiness. Were I stronger, it might be endured hopefully. But, being what I find myself, methinks I am of all mortals the most fit to die."

"You are fit for heaven without tasting death!" replied her husband. "But why do we speak of dying? The draught cannot fail. Behold its effect upon this plant."

On the window-seat there stood a geranium diseased with yellow blotches which had overspread all its leaves. Aylmer poured a small quantity of the liquid upon the soil in which it grew. In a little time, when the roots of the plant had taken up the moisture, the unsightly blotches began to be extinguished in a living verdure.

"There needed no proof," said Georgiana, quietly. "Give me the goblet. I joyfully stake all upon your word."

"Drink, then, thou lofty creature!" exclaimed Aylmer, with fervid admiration. "There is no taint of imperfection on thy spirit. Thy sensible frame, too, shall soon be all perfect."

She quaffed the liquid and returned the goblet to his hand.

"It is grateful," said she, with a placid smile. "Methinks it is like water from a heavenly fountain; for it contains I know not what of unobtrusive fragrance and deliciousness. It allays a feverish thirst that had parched me for many days. Now, dearest, let me sleep. My earthly senses are closing over my spirit like the leaves around the heart of a rose at sunset."

She spoke the last words with a gentle reluctance, as if it required almost more energy than she could command to pronounce the faint and lingering syllables. Scarcely had they loitered through her lips ere she was lost in slumber. Aylmer sat by her side, watching her aspect with the emotions proper to a man the whole value of whose existence was involved in the process now to be tested. Mingled with this mood, however, was the philosophic investigation characteristic of the man of science. Not the minutest symptom escaped him. A heightened flush of the cheek, a slight irregularity of breath, a quiver of the eyelid, a hardly perceptible tremor through the frame,—such were the details which, as the moments passed, he wrote down in his folio volume. Intense thought had set its stamp upon every previous page of that volume; but the thoughts of years were all concentrated upon the last.

While thus employed, he failed not to gaze often at the fatal hand, and not without a shudder. Yet once, by a strange and unaccountable impulse, he pressed it with his lips. His spirit recoiled, however, in the very act; and Georgiana, out of the midst of her deep sleep, moved uneasily and murmured as if in remonstrance. Again Aylmer resumed his watch. Nor was it without avail. The crimson hand, which at first had been strongly visible upon the marble paleness of Georgiana's cheek, now grew more faintly outlined. She remained not less pale than ever; but the birthmark, with every breath that came and went, lost somewhat of its former distinctness. Its presence had been awful; its departure was more awful still. Watch the stain of the rainbow fading out of the sky, and you will know how that mysterious symbol passed away.

"By Heaven! it is well-nigh gone!" said Aylmer to himself, in almost irrepressible ecstasy. "I can scarcely trace it now. Success! success! And now it is like the faintest rose color. The lightest flush of blood across her cheek would overcome it. But she is so pale!"

He drew aside the window curtain and suffered the light of natural day to fall into the room and rest upon her cheek. At the same time he heard a gross, hoarse chuckle, which he had long known as his servant Aminadab's expression of delight.

"Ah, clod! ah, earthly mass!" cried Aylmer, laughing in a sort of frenzy, "you have served me well! Matter and spirit—earth and heaven—have both done their part in this! Laugh, thing of the senses! You have earned the right to laugh."

These exclamations broke Georgiana's sleep. She slowly unclosed her eyes and gazed into the mirror which her husband had arranged for that purpose. A faint smile flitted over her lips when she recognized how barely perceptible was now that crimson hand which had once blazed forth with such disastrous brilliancy as to scare away all their happiness. But then her eyes sought Aylmer's face with a trouble and anxiety that he could by no means account for.

"My poor Aylmer!" murmured she.

"Poor? Nay, richest, happiest, most favored!" exclaimed he. "My peerless bride, it is successful! You are perfect!"

"My poor Aylmer," she repeated, with a more than human tenderness, "you have aimed loftily; you have done nobly. Do not repent that, with so high and pure a feeling, you have rejected the best the earth could offer. Aylmer, dearest Aylmer, I am dying!"

Alas! it was too true! The fatal hand had grappled with the mystery of life, and was the bond by which an angelic spirit kept itself in union with a mortal frame. As the last crimson tint of the birthmark—that sole token of human imperfection—faded from her cheek, the parting breath of the now perfect woman passed into the atmosphere, and her soul, lingering a moment near her husband, took its heavenward flight. Then a hoarse, chuckling laugh was heard again! Thus ever does the gross fatality of earth exult in its invariable triumph over the immortal essence which, in this dim sphere of half development, demands the completeness of a higher state. Yet, had Aylmer reached a profounder wisdom, he need not thus have flung away the happiness which would have woven his mortal life of the self-same texture with the celestial. The momentary circumstance was too strong for him; he failed to look beyond the shadowy scope of time, and, living once for all in eternity, to find the perfect future in the present.

www.ingramcontent.com/pod-product-compliance
Lightning Source LLC
Chambersburg PA
CBHW011512170626
46810CB00009B/3330